Mirth and Mayhem

A Story of Fantasy and Romance by Pan

by
Pollyann 'Pan' Castle

Mirth and Mayhem
©Pollyann Castle, 2020
All rights reserved.

Cover Illustration by:
Daniel Swanson

First printing, 2020

ISBN: 978-0-692-12237-2

Pollyann Castle
2020 Harbourside Drive
Longboat Key, FL 34228

Contents

Goodnight Moon

I said "Good Bye" to the moon last night. I was walking to my bedroom when I thought there was a reflection of a ceiling light on the sliding glass door. However, it was the early evening moon, shining a yellow-orange glow across the landscape. The moonlight transformed Sarasota Bay's waters into a shimmering reflection as brilliant as any diamonds and sapphires.

We all know that the moon's beams reflecting across the landscape revive memories of bygone days. These special memories endear us to the yellow ball in the night sky. It could be a lonely path illuminated by filtered moonbeams, or one of many nostalgic moments we have sat with a friend, a lover, a child or a companion pondering the magic of the moon.

So, here I was on my porch looking for that elusive face of the man in the moon. Unexpectedly, the ball started to bounce and roll in the sky. Round and round the ball rotated like a pick and roll in a basketball game. Then chunks disappeared like missing pieces of a pie. At this moment, I realized it was caused by my eyesight. To my ever growing list of farewells, the image of our earth's moon will always be in my heart and mind, but to the visual image, I must say "Good Night" and "Goodbye." I am trying to think of a redeeming grace, a replacement of this loss. This time it is just WHAT IT IS!!

Oh NO, I can still close my eyes and an image glows before me—it is the moon rising in the Eastern evening sky, promising the peaceful, magnificent face of the man in the moon smiling back at me!

This experience happened when I was 94. I am now 96 and in spite of struggling with macular degeneration I continue to seek joy in every day. I hope my "Ramblings and Rumblings" gathered here serve to inspire others to continue to live life to the fullest each day and choose Joy.

Ask A Question Each Morning

Yes, I moved to Florida in search of the "fountain of youth" just like everyone else…no luck. However, a discovery happened with the turn of the spiral in my 94th year. It came as a challenge put to me by an improbable mentor, a guru of sorts, who provoked me to change the question I ask myself upon rising every morning.

He helped me notice the question I was asking was, "Why AM I still here?" Day in and day out I was searching, "Why, why, why?" So negative. Gently, he suggested that age is simply a perspective and you can change it by changing your morning questions. I got curious.

Yes, it's like the story of baseball's Satchel Paige. When he was asked how old he was, Satchel Paige replied, "How old would you be if you didn't know how old you were?"

"What question could possibly do that?" I asked.

Here is the assignment he gave me to think about every morning:

"WHAT QUESTION CAN I ASK MYSELF TODAY THAT I HAVE NEVER, EVER ASKED MYSELF BEFORE?"

Be very aware of what follows as the day unfolds…because, he added, "A SURPRISE IS WAITING FOR YOU."

At first I thought, "Are you serious?" Living to be 94, there WAS NO question I had not already asked! But I loved the SURPRISE part! So I became willing to try.

And suddenly it came!

A question I had never asked myself before popped in and I recognized it as fresh and new. The answer became my immediate curiosity. I had to know!

It became a game with me. Some mornings I thought of two or three questions I had NEVER asked before. The best part was that something surprising DID come from it, not once, but EVERY TIME. I began to notice little things—something nice about the day, or the way the day flowed with a new ease or grace, or I became aware of the scent of a flower I had never really noticed before. It became a flow of sweet surprises, every day, of new ideas, new thoughts and new beginnings. The answers to my questions led me in new directions in my mind. I was THINKING again, not just complaining. My brain was becoming a source of new joys, even fascination. I felt younger!

You can too.

Getting To Know Me

My questions are not about learning new habits, changing everyday routines or behaviors. They are not a daily word, thought for the day or calendar momento with famous quote to ponder.

No, my philosophy of asking myself a morning question is to stimulate appreciation for life—for today, this moment.

How can we change? An attitude? A worry? A pain?

- IT'S NOW -

It's not a plan for today on living or a menu for dinner. These questions will introduce you to your inner self.

How do I perceive my life? How can I appreciate this new day, this moment in history? I think the greatest gift I can give myself is "appreciation," which can turn into gratitude. Next, imagination, then fascination and soon, before you know it, the impossible is possible. Or better yet, on this day there is a surprise waiting.

Just last week, I discovered that forgiveness for another or even oneself opens up a smile, a change in attitude and acceptance.

Forgiveness brings about a smile or a change. There will be a sunny day waiting for you.

My legacy IS this philosophy.

Discovery–
A Surprise Awaits

Yes, there is a fountain of youth for you.

It's in your smile.

It's in your heart.

It's fascination, jubilation.

It's in your recognizing

The blessings that come to you each day.

Why Should I Live In the Basement of My Thinking When I Can Live In the Penthouse?

I AM–ME–My being and my existence, my conscious mind, my body are no longer living on the same plane, plateau or level of life that I knew so well for the first 90 years of my life.

An awakening in my thinking put me on an elevator ride to another floor high in the sky. Here my life is joyful, happy, with a rosy radiance, a positive smile, a positive outlook; this joy seems to be ever constant, never leaving. It is with me in the morning, sleeping with me at night, reassuring me through a late afternoon.

UNTIL

Something from my past surfaces–a person's comment, a negative thought, some happening or circumstance, an event, on and on. It can be a word or deed. This throws me into a funk, a dark pouting place, a frustrating place, maybe an angry place

in my heart. Here I am once again, solidly standing in the basement of anxiety and depression.

LOOK AROUND–I've been here before.

I know this place.

Now, at this very moment, I HAVE to climb out of this
way of thinking, letting go of this idea, of this doubt and dis-
couragement. I will climb until I reach the Penthouse's beloved
BRILLIANCE, returning to the upper floor where I find pleas-
ant surprises carried along on the cool breeze of joy—light
hearted pleasures of living.

THIS IS MY NEW HOME!
UNTIL I AM...NO MORE

How Can I Change A Gloomy Day and Make It Happy?

❏　Believe that a surprise is waiting.

❏　Live in a positive attitude–look for the good.

❏　A passion or purpose brings joy.

❏　Negative thoughts or remarks keep sunshine from coming into your wonder.

❏　Make a difference. Find a pleasure, a smile, a laugh.

❏　Spreading happiness is contagious.

❏　Start a daily practice of contemplation, relaxation and appreciation.

❏　This is your life–no one else can live it for you, so look for the joy in being you.

Where Can I Go From Here?

This question has a very different answer for someone who is losing eyesight or who is blind. The loss of limbs, hearing, teeth or beauty is very different. Every day, every morning I check to see how much more eyesight, vision or distance has changed or disappeared—and it does incrementally.

NOW…where do I go from here? It has a very simple, positive solution: Keep courageous. Look for something to replace the loss or keep "climbing this mountain called LIFE." I must live and think like an inventor. Find something new to me that can replace the loss. Get plenty of rest and ample exercise. Invent—use my imagination. Live to find a new idea, new love or new joy each day.

There Is A Surprise Waiting For Me Today

Every morning when you wake up say this: "There is a Surprise waiting for me today. It will bring Fascination, Joy and Fresh Ideas."

Then ask: "Is there a Question that I have Never asked myself before?"

You will discover a SURPRISE IS WAITING!

What will it be today?

What is next?

It just takes being aware and paying attention to all the little things that happen throughout the day.

Is My Self Worth Tied Up In My Past Fortunes, Achievements, Choices, Or Future Hopes?

What I accomplished in life years ago is still pertinent today. It is in my DNA, my destiny. I can say, "I AM a Winner." Then I can ask myself: what have I contributed to my life that can open up a new vista, new horizon, new way of thinking? How can I value myself today—now? Can I think about myself in some new way?

In pondering these questions I found a burst of emotional energy and satisfaction. There was a release in my body that was rejuvenating. At the end of the day I found my worth to be a gift to myself. I am I, you are you. There is value in being, not just in achieving.

Each of us is unique. I spread my rainbow (share my inner self or 'soul' with others) through giving gifts (sometimes just a smile), helping others, showing compassion, giving time or attention.

How we each spread our unique rainbow and interact with others is life itself.

A Smile

My dance teacher, Tom, entered us in a Pro-Am Latin dance Championship competition. The age brackets ranged from age 30 to 60. I was in my late seventies. It was no surprise to us that I did not receive a call back after the first round of dances including Cha-Cha, Rumba, Samba, Paso Doble and Jive.

Tom and I returned to our table to await the placement awards to be announced at the end of the competition. After all awards were passed out, a judge from a prestigious New York City studio walked over to our table and said to me, "Pollyann, I would have given you first place if I were judging SMILES."

A smile will open hearts and doors.

A smile is the Grandest Good Morning!

Sportsmanship

Screams of disbelief and shock filled the auditorium where the North Carolina Tar Heels forfeited their supposed win and title of March Madness Basketball Champions for 2016.

Marcus Paige shot what everyone thought was the winning basket three seconds before the closing buzzer. As unexpected as a bolt of lightening, the Villanova Wildcat's ball flew across the boards, over the paint, in a direct arc slicing into the hoop just as the buzzer sanctioned its validity. Coaches stood in disbelief. Heartbroken, several players fell to their knees like rag dolls. The scoreboard verified it: Villanova 77, North Carolina 74. This was an unbelievable defeat.

After the game, Marcus Paige stood in front of the TV cameras defending his team. This ritual has been criticized and is now in review, but as a graduating senior at UNC, he admitted that the hurt and sorrow of defeat was a bitter pill. He then declared, "I had the time of my life. I would not have missed this opportunity to play ball with my teammates and work with the coaches, all before our loyal fans. I would not have missed playing this game for anything."

In the deepest defeat, a smile will lessen
the sting and helps to accept
disappointment.

Gratification is a smile from the heart.

Can I Live Today To the Fullest?

Can I live in the moment of now? How do I live in the moment of now?

"You cannot live tomorrow or yesterday, just now."

What Does "Stop To Smell the Roses" Really Mean?

Most people think it means to slow down and enjoy life. However, I think it may have deeper meaning–it may really be a way to discover a new idea.

To smell the perfume of flowers is to rejoice, relax and renew our spirit. Walk through your garden of ideas.

"Oh, here is a new flower I have not noticed before."

Inhale, relax, let the moment of silence awaken your imagination. It can create discovery, trust, connection, new ideas, hope, motivation, appreciation.

There is a flower waiting for you in your garden of life!

My Personal "Revolution"

The dictionary defines "revolution" as a rebellion, reversal, take-over, transformation, a pause.

My change has been to revolt against despair, disappointment and depression. I will not let it resurface. I do this by expressing, practicing and preaching the joy and fascination of living. The best lesson learned is that joy is a smile. Faith is revived every morning because we only live in this moment, the NOW. Let's celebrate Life!

Think how fortunate and blessed we are to recognize and embrace each new day. I can still make a difference. I can give a grin–get a smile. Hope is our springboard to NOW.

The time for courageous aging is NOW.

I Am Coming

Our minds and bodies are held together by what we know, have learned and live with now. Some of the patterns are old, worn out and need refreshing. Look at an old passion that can be revitalized, re-evaluated, rejuvenated. Our spirit needs a New Beginning; a Turning Point.

Where do I start? What kind of questions do I ask? It should be an open invitation to find me—to come in. Come In!

My first question is. "How do I look for a Turning Point and a New Beginning?"

It takes Silence where time slows down to a quiet, relaxed darkness where:

I can Think

I can Imagine

I can Muse

And "What If?"

If I can find Fascination, I can laugh. I can wait for Shock and Awe. That Surprise, breaking through the dawn of a new day, is the Sunrise heralding the coming of a new time—a new idea for ME.

Where is silence? How do I recognize Silence?

Close your eyes and ears—all senses to the outer world. Sit comfortably in silence and darkness—relax, drop your shoulders, release your body. Now clear your mind—don't think or get impatient. It may seem like preparation for a nap, but it is preparation for discovery, forgiveness and opening up your heart to receive goodness.

Silence is when all is empty, waiting for something creative to come into focus. It can be very powerful to quiet the mind and listen to the heart.

A Second Sunrise

SILENCE creeps in on little cat feet. It is the fog rolling in over the bay, blanketing my view with clouds that conceal. Are my thoughts and dreams shrouded in fog also? Must I search for that elusive change that could be a new beginning?

I have always embraced and toyed with the changes that an overcast day may illuminate. So, in my rumination and daydream like search, I remember another fog slipping over the prairie fields of flat lands and shrouding, silencing responses to what still lies out there. Finally, snuggling up against the waiting hills and dales, crags and canyons of majestic mountains, my answer comes through the fog.

Quiet silence is all around slowing down time and opening up space to a new Brilliance. Here is the New Beginning, The Turning Point. It is a thought, fresh and new, inspiring and achievable. It is a curtain rising on a drama that starts a dialogue of possibilities, bedded in fascination, fraught with probabilities.

It is the Morning Sunrise shining through the fog announcing a new day, my new day. Still knowing that I Am: not that I was or I have been, or what I can't see or I can't change, but it is me who is me.

I AM the Center

Of my Universe

Come to me, Brilliant newness

A SECOND SUNRISE

IS THE NEW BEGINNING

TO A

GLORIOUS

GOOD MORNING

I open the door to a new idea, never

Before acknowledged.

It is Coming-------------I am Coming.

Space: It Isn't Just "Out There"

We think of space as "looking to the heavens," further out to the moon, sun and stars. Space is the solar system, the galaxy, the black hole–mostly something far beyond our comprehension. Now look again. Space is part of the five elements as we know them: space, earth, air, water and fire. They belong to Earth, held under Earth's umbrella of gravity.

Let's look again. Space can be much more personal. It is the very area we live in for space is energy. It takes all five elements for us to survive on this planet Earth. We use space as a kind of signaling when we wave hello or goodbye. Everything that moves changes, displaces or rearranges energy. When intellect is attached to space, our personal lives, behavior and comprehension evolves into a clearer understanding of our life force here on Earth.

It is not only moving physical space for more room or change or challenge, but by using silence we can expand the space in our minds, our brains, our thoughts – our questions of "What's next? Why am I here? What can I do about it?" It's like trying on shoes until we find the perfect fit. First try on forgiveness, understanding, resolve, acceptance. Now peel away many layers until you come to the true life force—unconditional love.

Am I Living The Life I Want?

- ❑ Why or why not?

- ❑ What things can I change?

- ❑ What things do I have to accept because I have no control over them?

About Disappointment and Adversity

In the early morning hours before dawn there are times when my mind drifts back over my life. My memory settles on "what might have been." What could have been? How did I cope with adversity then? How did I truly survive so that I could smile again and bring a joyful moment to those that I love and those who counted on me and trusted me?

In these moments of doubt and disappointment, failures and lost goals, I can count the blessings and goodness that did befall me. As in a football game, there is the ever challenging goal line, another ten yards to cover. From age 70 to 100, we are in the Last Quarter of our lives. Let's play it like a football game. Let's play the game like the Fourth Quarter Folks. I want to contribute to this game called "LIVING."

When people hear that I am in my nineties they offer congratulations, then say, "I hope I can live to be 90!" They don't ask, "What is it like?" "What do you do?" "How do you cope?" My writing has been directed at other ninety year olds, but I find my message and musings appeal to any aged person who is struggling with a personal dilemma.

The challenge is: how can we take care of the responsibilities we have to ourselves and others who we care about?

So, back to those sorrowful moments in our memory banks. I would wager that for every disappointment you can find a positive outcome and accomplishment that still resonates today with you or someone you have touched or known. These personal talents and successes far outnumber the mental and emotional quarterback-like "sacks" we've endured.

Take time to reminisce, look for the gems. See if there are times you remember as sad or painful that have a silver lining.

Giving Gifts

- ❏ Have I missed an opportunity to say "thank you" for a kindness given to me?

- ❏ When was the last time I said thank you with more than a conditioned reply?

- ❏ What gifts (not necessarily material objects) can I give today?

- ❏ How does giving a gift make me feel?

- ❏ Do I receive the gifts of others with grace?

A Gift Nobody Wanted

A friend of mine was a Master Gardener. She had great success growing a wide variety of garden flowers.

One weekend she collected buckets of flowers, arranged them into bouquets and took them to her church. She decided this would be the perfect place to give them away and perhaps bring a smile to those accepting her gift.

The parishioners, however, all replied negatively when offered her gift.

"Oh, we're not going directly home."

"We're eating Sunday dinner out."

"Sorry, but we're allergic to flowers."

Standing alone in the church aisle she mused, "Now I know how Jesus felt when his teachings were dismissed and rejected."

What Am I Afraid of?

- How does this fear affect my progress through the day?
- How can I address a fear?

Move Over FEAR

I woke up with FEAR beside me this morning.

The loss of sight has crept into my bedroom, making objects look wavy and broken. I pushed fear away because I can find a much better acceptance to life than being afraid to face this new day—the future.

Fear comes upon me with a stranglehold.

How can I push it away? Do I really have the fortitude to address my problems, the sorrow for losses or depression?

My body is failing:

- ❏ My eyes
- ❏ My back
- ❏ My mobility is limited

Yet I sense I am more than this. Where within me must I look?

When our bodies fail us, we can turn to our minds.

My brain has so many untouched, unexplained avenues of exploration. The spotlight to find these new ideas and "another beginning" is through joy–a smile and laugh–not tears, depression or negative thoughts.

Move over, Fear, right now!

Breathe deeply, flex fingers, fan the shoulders back and chest out–headlights and high beams on. Seek out new rejuvenating energy within your body.

Step out on the arena of life for there is a surprise waiting!

Waiting for you in every thought is fascination, jubilation, appreciation and gratitude. We must never look back, pining for what was; whining about what could be or what could have been, what I expected, what I don't have, what should have been.

Turn to the East and look for the early morning sunrise where Hope rises and Change abounds.

Fascination awakens curiosity, a surprise awaits! I will once again ask myself, "What can I ask myself today that is new and challenging?" "What JOY can I receive from appreciation and gratitude?"

If I must say "Goodbye" to the Past, I say it with gratitude, for I have learned that:

I Love Life, and Life Loves Me!

STEP OUT ON THE ARENA OF LIFE.

YOUR FUTURE IS AN OPEN DOOR.

Is There a Worry Lurking In the Shadows of My Day Today?

- ❏ Am I aware of some old worry (or secret, or fear) I've carried around for a long time?

- ❏ Am I ready to let it go?

- ❏ Can I let it go? How?

Hasta La Vista Baby

Who could I be if I let my worst worry go? What if I changed a worry into a positive?" How would I feel? How could I do it? Do I really want to let go of the anger and discomfort, despair, disillusionments that I would be abandoning?

I wonder if I might like to HOLD A GRUDGE!!!

Well, if so, what happened to my question? My sermon? My mentor? My philosophy? The purpose of identifying a worry is to open up my heart, my life to Joy and Happiness, positive behavior and possibly Forgiveness.

I found a way to erase that worry from my conscious thinking. Write the problem on paper and place it in an envelope or write it in a notebook and hide it in the back of a drawer or on a closet shelf. When those familiar words of torment come to mind, say, "NO, I put you out of my view, my thoughts, and my mind." Move on.

After two or three shovings of those words away, I found a lighter mood, a lifting of my thoughts, a new happiness and joy of finding in myself a new person that I might like to get to know better!! I might become my own new BFF!

Are There Grudges
I Am Holding?

- ❏ Have I addressed them? Can I?
- ❏ What does it take to forgive?

On Forgiveness

To forgive is an internal, personal process. It takes willingness, intention, thought, courage, acceptance, release and the ability to move forward. It does NOT mean I come to accept what happened as "OK." It just means I choose to no longer let it have power over me and my thoughts, feeling and actions.

When my son, Bruce, was in the fifth grade he joined the beginner's basketball team. Finally, he was selected to play out the end of a game. To his great surprise, Bruce found the ball in his hands. The floor opened up before him with a clear path to the basket. He ran as hard as he could. With a swish he made the basket, thinking it had won the game. When he realized he shot the hoop on the opponent's end of the court giving the win to the other team, he was devastated.

Later in high school, because of his height at 6'3", many coaches asked Bruce to play basketball and he always refused. He never forgave himself for his mistake.

Sometimes the hardest person to forgive is me—myself.

Have I Been Criticized for Something I Did In Good Faith?

- ❑ How do I handle or deal with criticism?

- ❑ Can I learn something from it?

- ❑ Can I learn not to take it personally?

Shut The Door—
Don't Let the Flies In!

I have lived alone for many years enjoying the personal free-dom to make my own choices. I can select my preferred TV programs, set the furnace thermostat, turn lights off when I'm ready and never again hear the words repeated: "Will you shut the refrigerator door?"

As I was getting settled into my new home that is fur-nished with ultra-modern appliances, the refrigerator needed a lot of shelf adjustments. So, with little concern for escaping cool moist air, I placed and replaced the food until all fit the spaces provided. I took a moment to admire my handiwork, when an electronic alarm sounded over and over with urgency, BUZZ–BUZZ–BUZZ. Here was that same old warning: "Shut the door!"

BANG!

The Music Goes 'Round and Around

When was the last time someone commented on your driving skills? Could it have been a back seat driver with a heavy foot pushing an imaginary brake?

My husband and I drove by auto, round trip, from Illinois to Colorado for many years. I was expected to take my turn at driving, but my husband was so nervous with this that he would call out warnings and imagined mishaps every few miles.

I developed a plan that would challenge his need to be the one and only skilled best driver! As the miles slipped by on a stretch of deserted Kansas highway, I slowly allowed the car to drift over the center line. After another mile or so, I tested his patience by straddling the center line. In disbelief, he sat bold upright. "OK, pull over," he called out. "I'll do the driving."

All of the many trips thereafter, I could settle comfortably into a cushy back seat watching the scenery glide by. Even today I prefer riding in the back seat where I am reminded of the relaxed joy of travelling by passenger Pullman car or on a holiday tour bus excursion through uncharted vistas.

How times have changed. In a few years cars will be driving themselves. In this 21st Century we have GPS that gives routing to your desired destination. New automobiles have back-up cameras, lane departure warning signals, tire pressure monitors and other features that help us become safer drivers. There is no more stopping at filling stations to ask for directions! Or how about backing out of a parking spot? No more dangerous encounters with telephone poles!

I wonder if I will miss being a human back seat driver?

Don't Rain On My Parade

When Debra, my daughter-in-law, and I were gathering material for my first book "Grin & Giggle," we visited places in Loveland, Colorado that brought back nostalgic memories for me so we could take photos. We went to Washington Elementary School where I attended third grade. I then took her to the First Presbyterian Church on Fourth Street. I wanted to show her the room where I attended Sunday school as a five year old.

As we entered the church, the organist was rehearsing a hymn on the gleaming pipe organ. Debra and I slid into one of the pews at the back of the church to absorb the beauty of the scene and the music.

A surge of recollection and nostalgia enveloped me. I said, "Debra, I've been here before. It was Easter Sunday 1943. Because war rationing was in full force, new clothes were scarce – no new Easter bonnet, dress or suit. I did manage to wear a new blouse under my threadbare chocolate brown suit." This memory brought a rush of gratitude to me. Just then the pastor's wife came up to us, inquiring as to our intent.

I shared the story of my joy for having something new to wear to the Easter service back in 1943. Looking at me for a long moment and nodding, she then asked, "Yes, and do you remember what the pastor's sermon was about?"

I immediately felt like she'd doused me with a bucket of cold water. I decided I would not let her take away my joy, but it took some inner work to let go and regain my happy thoughts.

Do I Resist Change or Challenge As I Get Older?

I f so, why?

Some changes are sudden, unexpected and outside my control. How do I deal with changes imposed on me?

Change is a universal phenomenon. Life only moves forward with change.

Dark Side

There is a dark side to reaching 90. Life as we know it, lived it and loved it will change. BE PREPARED! It's coming. It will take acknowledgement, patience and a sense of humor or humility to create a new beginning. Recognize that there will be CHANGE: physical, mental and/or emotional.

But the GOOD NEWS: there is a beginning point for everyone's acceptance. It's what fascinates, stimulates, titillates, and awakens my mind, my brain, my senses, my observations. I can ruminate, stretch my imagination, draw and lift energy, power and force. It's named ME–POLLYANN.

It's named YOU.

Challenge Vs Change

Am I grieving for something I cannot have?

Has life changed so much that I feel defeated, depressed and despondent?

I have always met life's challenges with courage, determination and resolve. Is it age that clouds my vision and purpose? Could my worries be inflamed by poor health and pain? I cannot take care of my daily chores. Many of my life long friends have gone or moved away. I cannot drive any more, so my joy of discovery diminishes.

What do I have left in old age (I am now 96), that I can count on?

There must be something new that I can develop to sustain the joy of living. We must follow the flow of living–the everyday change in our mental, physical and psychological being with each moment that ticks by. Our age moves along, clocking us into another day, a new year that could add up to a decade. Even when change brings imperfections, impermanence and unpredictability, we can meet it with grace and courage.

Pining for what was, whining about what could be or what it could have been, what I expected, what I don't have, what should have been, is not productive. Acceptance is key.

Turn to the East and look for the early morning sunrise where hope rises, change abounds, fascination awakens curiosity and there is a surprise waiting. I will once again ask myself, "What can I ask myself today that is new and challenging?" What joy can I receive from appreciation and gratitude?

TEACH ME SOMETHING NEW TODAY.

How Hard Is It To Replace An Old Idea or Habit With a New One?

❏   Does my old behavior feel more familiar or comfortable?

❏   How often do I challenge myself to try something new?

I use my imagination!

❏   Memorize poetry phrases

❏   Whistle

❏   Invent dance steps

❏   Do simple aerobic moves

❏   Remember the lyrics to songs I have loved

Go Granny Go!

Is she still chasing rainbows?
Is she still dancing her dance?
Is she still falling in love?
Can she still drive her little red
roadster all over town?
Yes! Here she comes,
Give her a salute!
Here's to the little old lady
On the road again.
Go Granny Go!

Do I Find Myself Whining Or Complaining Daily?

❏ How can I change my thinking?

Mr. Happy

Mr. Happy first announced high tea and garden parties at my home in Loveland, Colorado. He moved to Florida with me and he found a new calling. A neighbor of mine was very negative and constantly complained about her health.

Mr. Happy began sharing happy thoughts and messages in the hallway for passersby to see. At first his messages had a food theme, but they evolved over time. He shared joy and good cheer throughout the year.

I enjoyed the challenge of thinking up messages for Mr. Happy to share and the conversations that were started by his presence.

My neighbor eventually moved away, but Mr. Happy still shares positive messages from time to time.

There is happiness
out there,
You just have to look
for it !!
HAPPY DAYS AHEAD!

THERE IS A
RA NBOW OF
HAPPINESS...
Joy is the Pot of
Gold !!

Survival

How can we move forward in old age? Our bodies are tired, perhaps opportunities have passed us by. Yet we are still here. We can still wake up each morning eager to greet a new day. Maybe there will be a surprise waiting. Could it be that my pain has diminished or that there is a phone message or a letter in the mail box?

There is a calm, peaceful joy that I can bring into my new day. It is to be appreciative. It takes courage, consideration and contemplation to welcome today, another morning with hope, love and trust.

How can I do this? Not all mornings are positive, but I do have courage and curiosity to check out hidden ideas. Like "stop and smell the roses," here is the moment to try out a new idea. We can look to nature where renewal and rejuvenation suggest belief, hope and renewal.

We still have a bag of tricks. Think of it as a lottery where you can pull out a new idea, a forgotten exercise. Let me introduce you to practices and activities I have found that help me meet the challenges today's sunrise may present. Yes, there is a silver lining and it's much better than whining.

The answer is in your heart, in my heart where peace and happiness can only come from our personal dedication to living each day, each moment with positive energy. Let's start with a smile, a twinkle in the eye, a little giggle!

❑ Living with a purpose…

When adversity appears how do I cope? Do I whine, complain and blame others? Do I really know how to move forward with positive vibes and renewed believable energy?

❑ Life is inflicted with imperfections and impermanence, all wrapped in unpredictability. It is how I meet and adjust to these life changing moments that I must understand, interpret and ingest. I must find the path that leads to a motion forward in my energy, my needs, my happiness and even survival.

❑ Be Positive…

❑ Pundits give advice on how to move forward with love, wealth, good health, fun and joyous behavior. All good advice until you reach the last few years left on earth. It's the last quarter, and I'm striving to reach the goal line with GRACE.

❏ How I do this has a different game plan than the one
I have always practiced. Now my goal is to live each
day in good humor, overlooking and ignoring nagging
pain–embracing daily chores that took previously two
minutes and now consume hours. I am no longer trying to create a new world, but to survive in the one I
have with Joy and Grace.

How To Stay Positive

Pave every step forward with positive thinking or you will lose ground. This means there can be no opening for depression and negativity. Negative thinking brings about defeat. Stay out of the basement of thinking. I can't say my essay "Why Should I Live in the Basement of My Thinking…" can miraculously take me out of the basement to joyous living, but I can be aware and prepare for "peaceful" thinking and behavior called happiness.

BELIEVING IS ACHIEVING

How Can I Minimize the Physical Pain I Feel Today—Right Now?

This is an exercise that I use:

- ❑ I close my eyes and breathe deeply.

- ❑ I yawn three times

- ❑ I visualize myself sending the pain or physical discomfort in a stream or ribbon of energy flowing out into the universe (space).

- ❑ I listen to music.

- ❑ I find an activity I enjoy to distract my mind.

What do <u>you</u> do to minimize your pain?

It Still Takes Patience

Take control of your disability. Of course if you are or have been confined to your bed, most of your time is given over to getting well, feeling better–working to conquer that disability, that illness. As you begin to feel better, you begin to awaken again. Your mind, thoughts and emotions begin to awaken and ask, "What can I do? How can I spend my day? What's next?" Then if you are a senior in your 90's, your next question is, "I wonder how much time I have left? or Can I finish my project?"

Here's my answer: Don't worry, don't fret. It does not matter how much time is left. What matters is that I feel productive, alive and joyous to express the fascination of living. What is here for me today? Is there a surprise waiting? I can begin another day with that positive sunrise of hope. Yes, here is a new day rising.

Good morning!

Do I Feel Lonely?

What do I do to abate loneliness?

My answer to this question has changed with my ever changing physical ability, sight and living situation.

How can you reach out to others? Are you able to get to club meetings? Do you have children or grandchildren that live nearby? Do you have neighbors? Is there a library nearby you can visit regularly?

If you are housebound, do you have a computer or phone to connect with friends or family?

Do you have hobbies or interests to keep you busy? Reading? Arts and crafts? Games or puzzles? Sports?

Other ideas:

- ❏ Collect photos into collages or albums.
- ❏ If you have travelled, pinpoint the places you have visited on a map or a pegboard.
- ❏ Make a collage of your achievements, interests, family.
- ❏ Write a gratitude journal and add something every

day.

- ❑ Keep a questions journal and come up with a new question each morning to ask yourself that you have never asked before.
- ❑ Use your imagination to come up with new endings to Fairy Tales or Nursery Rhymes.

YOU DESERVE A DONUT

Do I Have a Talent or Interest I Have Never Used or Explored?

Is there a talent or hobby from my past I can rework, refresh, renew and enjoy today–perhaps in a new way?

As a librarian by profession, I have enjoyed story telling and writing for many years. In the 60's, I wrote a number of short stories and even a play which was produced for the Illinois Sesquicentennial. I renewed this interest and wrote my first book "Grin & Giggle" in my early 90's.

I listened to basketball on the radio as a young girl and teenager because it was a passion of my Mother's. I renewed this interest and became more familiar with the colleges, teams, mascots, conferences and tournaments. I started a mug collection and began following the wins and losses, leading up to March Madness. Don't try to contact me in March! I am passionate about college basketball!

Sweet Sixteen

Basketball's Sweet Sixteen was created for high school competition from 1923-1944. Kentucky, Indiana and Illinois supported this system until March Madness embraced college basketball. Early on, any size school was eligible to compete. One year, a southern Illinois rural high school with 98 students won the Sweet Sixteen. My mother loved basketball, so every March we huddled around the radio for the broadcasts.

By the time I was 10 years old, I had a new baby brother. The depression was at its most challenging, a 25¢ movie ticket was too costly, but high school basketball was still available entertainment. Distances, weather and the cost of gasoline often prohibited attending the games so consequently, entertainment centered around the radio.

Gather Around The Radio

When the Illinois prairie "January thaw" brought rain, fog and above freezing temperatures producing soft, slippery, rutty rural gravel farm roads we turned to the radio.

Cabin fever could be in full force by February, so Basketball's Sweet Sixteen broadcasts satisfied our family's passion for the high school sporting event. My mother loved basketball so these broadcasts attracted us to gather around the radio, like moths to a night light. I could stretch out on the floor in front of the radio. Mother and Daddy leaned in from each side, ears close to the speaker so as to catch every nuance and change in the action or score of that game.

One particular year, I remember my mother rooting for a small team from southern Illinois. The team numbered 6 or 7 players to no more than 12. Yes, it was one of the smallest schools to compete against any city team. Could this have been the winning team in the record book? Perhaps, for I do remember that the team from a southern Illinois school won.

I like to think that my passion today for March Madness

comes from rekindling these earlier memories from my child-

hood.

Will This Morning's News Change or Impact My Day?

I cannot do anything about daily current events in the news, even though they can influence or shape the direction of my life and what choices I make.

I <u>CAN</u> make a difference in my own attitude, thinking and choices.

WHAT'S NEW?

How Can I Accept Change?

- ❏ Will changing my attitude or perspective make a difference?

- ❏ Does change offer more:
  - ❏ Tolerance?
  - ❏ Understanding?
  - ❏ Appreciation?
  - ❏ Gratitude?
  - ❏ Jubilation?

On Winning

Why do I tear up when I watch a closely fought basketball game, one where the outcome is not really critical to me? It's more than winning or losing, or numbers on the scoreboard. It's the grit, will, pounding out every last ounce of strength and determination that will carry the spirit to the finish line.

Suddenly I am aware that I, too, have a shortness of breath, a quickness and pounding in my chest, a clapping of sweaty palms. To see the teams struggle to reach the goal, the highest score, the magic numbers that altogether spell success, a winner—you did it—gives me a jolt of energy.

In that moment I ask myself, "What am I doing? Why does this mean so much to me?" The answer comes as swiftly as the swoosh of the winning basket. This struggle represents my struggle, my victory as a ninety year old soul who is still playing the game.

Why do I compare winning a game such as basketball to how I feel today? When there is a competition there is always a winner and loser. No matter how important the final outcome seems, it is whether we win or lose with courage and grace that *REALLY* matters.

Do I Find Myself Always Saying Goodbye?

❏   How can I say goodbye with grace?

Where Is It?

Pollyann 'Pan' Castle

Don't worry,

Don't fret my Pet,

You will find it.

No, where is it?

Whether it's underwear, an old coat or a long worn out pair of

shoes.

It should be where I left them, in the dresser drawer next to the

window.

Look around,

We no longer live in that room or that house. Nevertheless, our memory and habits return to another time and place.

Don't worry,

Don't fret my Pet,

You are OK.

It just takes a few moments to leave our familiar beloved past and return to this moment, the present.

Don't worry,

Don't grieve,

Just believe, my friend.

Believe that a moment of forgetfulness is a flashback in nostalgia.

Saying Goodbye

I have discovered in my 90's that saying "Goodbye" does not always bring final closure. With a positive attitude it can mean change, a new beginning, a different perspective. However, it may take courage, imagination and humor. Start with a smile, for that represents a new sunrise, a new idea and another chance.

A goodbye can seem so final, but it can also herald a new beginning, a new idea. It may take a little time for me to realize it.

I started competitive ballroom dancing when I was 62, winning trophies and first place honors for 20 years. Finally my knees gave out and my back said, "enough of this!" Saying goodbye to the lifestyle of glamour, glitter and glitz, it took several years to overcome my grief and feeling of loss.

There was a new beginning waiting for me, however, with the encouragement of the Loveland Rose Society and District members of the American Rose Society. I found a new purpose in the circle of appreciation, gratification, friendship and sharing. There is constancy in appreciating flowers, specifically roses, for me. In my garden of 160 rose bushes, I learned that a goodnight kiss and caress responds with "Love a rose and it will love you in return."

At 90 I wasn't ready to give up showing rose arrangements so I went back to class and became a certified National Judge for flower arrangements for the American Rose Society.

In 2015 I agreed that it was too difficult to care for my very large home and garden–coupled with Colorado's winter weather. So, I had another goodbye to address. I discovered that this time, I could say "so long" with anticipation of a new beginning–looking forward to a different life. This time I tried to say "goodbye" with understanding and grace.

In 2015 I wrote my first book "Grin & Giggle" which was published in 2016. It was a way to share my life and memories with others, hoping it would inspire them to take a look back and remember the good things, to find the hidden silver linings in their own lives.

A few years ago, my words of optimism and purpose ran into an unexpected change and challenge for my future–I was diagnosed with macular degeneration. So, I had to ask myself, "Well, can I really apply and practice my philosophy of hope, new beginnings and find a project with a purpose?" Then I said to myself, "Hey Pollyann, why are you moping around over what you can't do? You have it good. I know you appreciate your blessings. Why does it seem like you are…WHINING?"

I can answer: Yes, but how many times do I have to say goodbye? It seems I am always adjusting to health problems: loss of mobility, diminished hearing and now loss of sight.

Oh hey, Pollyann, you are 96. You are blessed with a strong body, you have no major health issues and you have people who love you. You are revered for your positive attitude and welcoming smile. You can keep on going with grace.

A few days ago I got some news that encouraged me. My philosophy works! I went to the eye doctor for a checkup. I wanted a progress report on my macular degeneration because I hadn't been in for two years. The report: my eyes continue to deteriorate (thankfully it is progressing slowly). However, my peripheral vision is holding. Because of my positive attitude and willingness to learn I have found a way to use my peripheral vision to compensate partially for my loss.

My dear friends, face your demons! Know that a second sunrise will shine on another happy, positive day.

Have I Seen This Day Before?

Pollyann 'Pan' Castle

As sun rises on a new dawn

It heralds the beginning of another day,

A day so new

So fresh with possibility.

But wait, I've been here before.

I know this day.

It's the same as yesterday,

What am I waiting for?

When the sun smiles back at me

Is he tired too?

Has he been here before—

Last year? Perhaps a decade ago.

Imagine that the same sunrise

Gave its first light

To Columbus seeing land—

THAT was a new beginning!

Yes, every sunrise wakes anew

Fresh opportunities, new thoughts, blessings.

Why, of course!

This morning's sunrise is just for me.

Look again,

For it is happiness that I see.

Fairy Tales, Nursery Rhymes and Poems

Coming up with and writing 21st century endings to fairy tales became a way for me to use my creativity and imagination. I started with the idea of writing a story in the style of a Greek myth which evolved into my book "Mirth and Mayhem." Then I looked for another genre to work with. It just came to me to change Fairy tales to a modern (and sometimes surprise) ending.

Why Fairy tales? Fairy tales teach life lessons, such as: our actions have consequences. Some offer hope: good can conquer evil, enemies can be vanquished. Fairy tales expand our view of what is possible. They are short and can be finished in one sitting. Finally, they open our minds and imaginations to fantasy.

The Clint Eastwood movie "The Beguiled" (1971) in which his character was fed poison mushrooms gave me the idea for the first story I wrote, "Little Red Riding Hood." I then had the idea to do the same thing with nursery rhymes and eventually branched out to other poems, as well as writing some original poems.

My mother was a practiced storyteller and dinner party table conversation was her platform. I think these stories and poems could have been perfect for her use.

When I married, my husband Dick and I enjoyed entertaining. I did all of the cooking and as I went to and from the kitchen serving guests, Dick was expected to keep the table conversation lively. He could mesmerize guests with an unexpected rendition of Lewis Carroll's "Jabberwocky," or recite parts of Chaucer's "Canterbury Tales" spoken in the old English of the 1600's.

These stories and poems could have expanded his repertoire.

I hope you enjoy the results.

Come Out to Play

(Retold from an 18th century English

nursery rhyme)

Girls and boys come out to play,

The moon doth shine as bright as day.

Leave your supper and leave your sleep,

And come with your pillows into the street.

Come with a whoop, come with a call,

Come with good will or not at all.

Up the ladder and over the wall.

Here we land before a big screen,

It's a drive-in theater where people pay.

They come to relax after a strenuous day,

Watching movies from their cars,

While we sit on our pillows under the stars.

Jack Be Nimble

(Retold from a 19th century English

nursery rhyme)

Jack be nimble,

Jack be quick.

Jack jumped over

The candle stick

But by accident

His foot knocked

Over the candle,

Sending it rolling

Across the floor,

Setting curtains aflame.

The flames consumed

Not only his house,

But the entire block.

Upon investigation,

The police arrested him

As an arsonist.

His court date was set.

When he walked into the courtroom,

He came face to face

With the presiding judge,

"Judge Judy!"

Humpty Dumpty

(Retold from an 18ᵗʰ century nursery rhyme)

Humpty Dumpty sat on a wall.

Humpty Dumpty had a great fall.

All the King's horses and all the King's men

Could not put Humpty together again.

But wait, not far away

There was a convention of doctors and surgeons.

Hearing the commotion,

They hurried to the accident scene.

"Why, we can repair him."

So Humpty was off to the hospital.

After a surprisingly short recovery period,

Humpty was completely restored

To his original egg-shaped self.

The very next morning,

Humpty hurried back to the Palace,

Scaled the wall, crossed the moat

And headed directly to the Palace kitchen.

The Head Chef appeared to be waiting for him

And called out,

"Why, good morning Mr. Egg. We have been waiting for your return."

"Great," Humpty replied. "What are we having for breakfast today?"

Chef gave a puzzled frown and then with purpose in his voice, he called out,

"Why, you of course, Mr. Egg!"

Four and Twenty Black Birds

(SING A SONG OF SIXPENCE)

(Retold from an 18th century nursery rhyme)

Sing a song of sixpence

A pocket full of rye.

Four and twenty black birds

Baked in a pie.

When the pie was opened

The birds began to fly.

Wasn't that a dainty dish

To set before his eye?

The King was in his counting house

Counting out his money.

The Queen was in the parlor

Eating bread and honey.

The maid was in the garden

Hanging out the clothes.

Along came a black bird

And snipped off her nose.

The King then saw it as his duty

To restore the maiden's former beauty.

He took her to a plastic surgeon

Who soon had her looking new again.

Now she sits in the counting house

Counting out the King's money.

The Queen is in the garden now

Hanging out the clothes.

Along came a black bird

Calling, "And so it goes!"

The Tortoise and The Hare

(Retold from the original tale by Aesop)

The hare and the tortoise were at a rest stop when a van with a loud speaker and blaring horn drove by advertising the Boston Marathon. This piqued the hare's interest for he was sure he could win it. He and the tortoise both entered the race in the category of pets and children.

The momentous day arrived and the race started. The hare realized he was way ahead of his opponents and decided he was so far ahead, he could sit down in the grass beside the trail. He soon fell asleep.

When the hare woke, the trail was empty and the streets were quiet. Realizing he was left behind, he pulled a cell phone from his pocket and quickly called for an Uber driver to pick him up. His plan worked like a charm. He exited the car just far enough from the finish line so he could sprint across the goal line, expecting first place.

Finally, almost all the runners had finished the race. The

tortoise, however, was no where to be seen. The runners were waiting patiently and far, far in the distance police sirens screamed for attention. They were escorting the last participant to finish the race.

There was a surprise for all as the judges decided that the tortoise should be selected as winner of the race for he represented the old adage:

"Slow and steady sets the pace.
Slow and steady can win the race!"

The Little Mermaid

(Retold from the

Hans Christian Anderson fairy tale)

One early morning the swim coach for the U.S. women's swim team was putting his team through their paces in Denmark's Copenhagen harbor. Their vigorous splashing attracted the Little Mermaid who lived in the harbor waters. She soon began to imitate all of the intricate diving positions and out-distanced the lap swimmers to the point that her antics attracted the attention of the swim coach.

The team members embraced her and the coaches trained her so that she was soon ready to enter the next Summer Olympics to be held in Copenhagen. For the diving competition, she entered the water with the straightest legs, with extended toes and minimum splash. Her swimming laps were fastest and varied. Yes, she won many gold medals, rivaling Michael Phelps and other champions.

Today if you look very carefully, you may see the Little

Mermaid sunning on her rock in Copenhagen Harbor with a cluster of gold medals hanging around her neck shining ever so brightly in the sunlight.

Little Red Riding Hood

(Retold from a tale by Charles Perrault)

Little Red Riding Hood and her Granny owned and operated a health center. Little Red roamed the forest looking for roses, roots, berries and mushrooms which pharmaceutical houses tested and developed into new and innovative holistic medicines.

One day, while Granny was working in her patch of medicinal marijuana, the front doorbell rang. Hurrying to the door, she found Mr. Wolf weak, disheveled and near exhaustion. "Please ma'am, may I come in to rest?" he asked.

"Why?" Granny questioned.

"The old days when wolves were feared are long gone. Farmhouses have become suburbs and cities. I have no place to go, no food to eat and no one fears me anymore," he lamented.

Granny was of that last older generation that took strangers into their care. She took Mr. Wolf into her home. Soon with a vegan diet, exercise and double doses of the newest medicinal roots and potions, Mr. Wolf's eyes became bright and his responses quickened. Granny was overjoyed for he appeared to be the perfect "guinea pig" for her potions. It did not take long for Mr. Wolf to adapt to their 21st century philosophy of living.

After much searching in the forest, Little Red returned to Granny's with her forest bounty. Calling to Mr. Wolf to come along, Granny ran to help Little Red unload her red roadster. Now "Wolfy" had never seen such a magnificent automobile. It ran on electricity, could maneuver the road by GPS, the console had every gadget imaginable and the bucket seats were as cushy as clouds. He lingered over the car long after it was emptied, amazed and dazed.

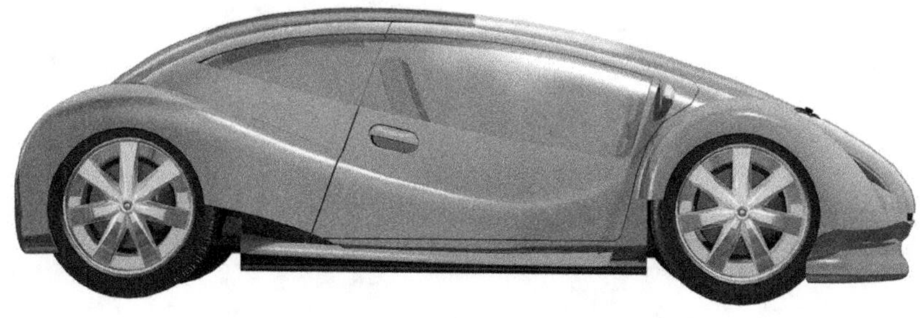

That evening to celebrate Little Red's joyous return, Granny called all to feast on a sumptuous vegan dinner. When the ladies went to the kitchen to prepare dessert, Mr. Wolf left the dining room. Suddenly the two ladies heard a loud sound, a backfire blast, squealing tires and a scatter of gravel. As they hurried to the front door, they saw Mr. Wolf speeding away in Little Red's brand new roadster.

"Oh Granny, what can we do?" wailed Little Red. Comforting Little Red with her arm around her shoulder, Granny said, "I saw an unusual glimmer in Wolfy's eyes. He seemed agitated and anxious. I know that behavior." Then with a loud shout out, Granny confessed, "He won't get far for I fed him poisonous mushrooms for supper!"

Goldilocks and The Three Bears

(Retold from a fairy tale first published
by Robert Southey)

I'll wager you didn't know that Goldilocks was on a mission. She had a problem to solve.

It was reported that there was a little house in the woods where three bears lived. Here she stood ringing the door bell, but soon found the door ajar so in she went. She sat in each of the three chairs of assorted sizes, then moved to the kitchen where three bowls of porridge remained from the bears' breakfast. Next she found three beds, so she settled down in the smallest one to wait for the bears to return and she fell asleep.

When the bears returned after a day of working the neighborhood, they spread their treasures on the dining room table. The bears' shouts of glee and success woke Goldilocks out of her slumber. She ran downstairs shouting, "Put your hands up! You're all under arrest. Don't move, I have you covered."

Surprised and bewildered, Father Bear questioned, "Who are you?"

"I'm an FBI agent. You are under arrest." Before the bears could resist, she cuffed them together while reading them their rights.

"Hey!" shouted Mother Bear. "We're innocent. What proof do you have that we burglar and terrorize neighborhoods?"

"Oh," she replied. "I have the evidence. Your fingerprints are all over the chairs. I found DNA in your bowls of porridge and lastly, you shed bits of fur in your beds."

When the littlest bear protested, Goldilocks reached out and pulled a zipper under the bear's chin and it opened up a Halloween bear costume. At her orders, three men stepped out of their fur suits while removing their bear heads.

"Sorry, the jig is up boys, she has us."

Goldilocks called out to her backup partner in triumph, "Book 'em Danno!"

The Three Little Pigs

(Retold from an English folk tale)

The three Pig brothers were gathered at Little Pig III's spacious brick house to watch the celebrated Super Bowl game between the Fairyland Wolverines and Black Forest Bears. It was not easy for the pigs to watch the anointed Wolverines play today, because decades earlier a quarterback named Mr. Big Bad Wolf had terrorized the pigs and their neighbors with mayhem and destruction.

The doorbell began to ring incessantly and deliberately nonstop.

When Little Pig III answered the door he came face to face with the big bad wolf from years past. Mr. Wolf appeared smaller, almost shriveled, meek and dressed in an old heavily worn business suit. He was carrying an oversized scuffed briefcase.

"Hello, I'm Mr. 'Big Bad' Wolf. I'm here as your friend and want to insure that you have a better life," he said as he pushed his way into their living room. "I want to make amends for the way I treated you in the past. I have here in my briefcase a way whereby you can protect your property and yourselves to live a worry free and happy life to end of your days," he concluded. He did seem sincere, so they sat down to hear more.

In his earlier years Mr. Big Bad Wolf was a linebacker with the Fairyland Wolverine football team. Then he practiced his bombastic "do it my way" attitude toward others whom he encountered. Now, decades later, he found himself out of step, left behind and struggling in an unfamiliar world of computers, congested highways and indifferent citizens, possibly contemplating his future in a retirement home. He appeared to the pigs to be compassionate and genuine.

Turning to Little Pig I, Big Bad cautioned in a persuasive voice, "You need to find protection from household catastrophes such as high winds so your straw house won't blow away." He really was taking a chance here, hoping the pig would not remember his threatening words of, "I'll huff and I'll puff until I blow your house down!"

Turning to Little Pig II, he reminded him of the time a stranger threatened to eat him up. "You need health insurance with protection from disease; a life policy that also adds the security of a burial clause," Big Bad urged. "And you, my dear friend, Little Pig III, absolutely need protection from a predator climbing down your chimney or burglars stealing your valuables and vandalizing your home."

After a short deliberation the three little pigs quickly took out the insurance policies believing this could provide relief from fear and anxiety in their future.

"Well, I must go. I hope you three have a long, prosperous, healthy and happy future. Remember what I say: With the right thinking and attitude you can live a life of happiness."

The three pigs settled down to watch the game feeling safe and secure. The doorbell rang again. This time it was a neighbor with the newspaper. The headline read:

Beware, Warning

WANTED: Big Bad Wolf

For scamming seniors.

Their money gone, but their lives still intact, the three pigs vowed to enjoy watching the game and not open the door anymore. They did feel grateful anyway, for they still had the one thing that brought them Joy–EACH OTHER.

All's Well That Ends Well!

Jack And Jill

(Retold from an 18th century English nursery rhyme)

Jack and Jill went up the hill

To fetch a pail of water.

Jack fell down

And broke his crown.

And Jill came tumbling after!

Then up Jack got and off did trot

As fast as he could caper,

To old Dana Dob, who patched his nob

With vinegar and brown paper.

'Twas time for Jill to create

A helmet made of plastic.

Designed for Jack and all to wear

Stretching like elastic.

Her business idea was ever so new

Sales success just grew and grew.

Soon TV's Shark Tank became their target,

Introducing them to a million dollar market!

Hansel and Gretel

(Retold from the original tale by the Grimm Brothers)

The original "Hansel and Gretel" fairy tale was created and written by the German Brothers Grimm. Their story centers around hunger and poverty of the Middle Ages. Unfortunately, poverty is still with us today in the 21st century.

Hansel and Gretel lived with their parents on the edge of a dense forest. They were always hungry and scavenging for food. One day their parents decided to send the children into the forest in search of food. They soon became disoriented, then lost. Darkness was descending when they came upon a little hut that remarkably was made of bread, rolls, cookies and sweets. They immediately started to nibble, then tear off hunks of siding to satisfy their hunger.

From inside a voice called out, "Who's there?" They had no intention of running away for the little hut offered a solution to their plight. Hansel replied, "It's two kids from the city. We're lost, may we come in?" This was a gift to the little old witch for it was her duty to supply "child labor" to her clients. Just inside were cages where the witch held her captures.

Hansel was a very bright young man. When he saw this situation, he quickly pulled out his cell phone and called 911. Soon the police arrived. Recognizing the old woman was one of the 10 most wanted criminals, they took her off to prison in chains. As she passed Hansel and Gretel, she snarled "You two can have this old place for it will come to no good."

Hansel and Gretel, left with the property, took a look

around and found baking ovens in the back. They were so hungry that they took some pita bread, covered it with a topping and popped it into the oven. Suddenly Gretel had a vision. "Let's cook pies in the oven. We have the hut, we can make and sell these pies as pizzas here in the hut."

Their success spread as they franchised their "Pizza Hut" idea. Their restaurants, huts and drive-ups grew into a national success turning the witch's prophecy to a positive force. Just look for their sign that says,

> "Come get Gretel's Griddled Pizzas.
> Say it twice and earn another slice!"

There Was An Old Woman Who Lived In A Shoe

(Retold from an 18th century nursery rhyme)

There was a little old woman who lived in a shoe.

She had so many children she didn't know what to do.

She gave them some broth without any bread.

She kissed them all soundly and put them to bed.

It soon became quite clear as her family grew,

She suddenly knew just what to do.

Working together, she and her kids

Put together a plan for remodeling old shoes.

The uniqueness of this project soon hit the news,

A little old woman so dear

Who made Flipping a new career.

Now she is known as the FLIPPING QUEEN OF THE YEAR!

Mary Had A Little Lamb

(Retold from a 19th century American nursery rhyme)

Mary had a little lamb,

Its fleece was white as snow.

And everywhere that Mary went,

The lamb was sure to go.

One day, they met Mistress Mary

Who was often quite contrary.

They asked her, "How does your garden grow?"

"With silver bells and cockle shells

But Fleecy White ate the pretty maids

That sat in a row."

Next it was to market, to market

To sheer little lamb's coat.

But with a stubborn pout,

Little Lamb did speak out,

"No, not now, no, no, NO!"

Just watch for clues

For now I'm in my Terrible Twos!"

Cinderella

(Retold from a tale by Charles Perrault)

I think we all know the story of Cinderella and how she was mistreated by her stepmother and two stepsisters. Remember how the fairy godmother set her up with a pumpkin carriage, fine horses and outfitted Cinderella in a stunning white dress, glittering with golden stars? Her hair was piled high on top of her head and it, too, was sprinkled with stars. On her feet were tiny glass slippers with diamonds in the heels. When Cinderella arrived at the ball, everyone turned to look at the unknown beauty who arrived so unexpectedly and uninvited.

Now we all know the events that ensured the fairytale fate of Cinderella, but there is a back story to this tale. It is soon to break in all of our newspapers, *Business Week* and *Wall Street Journal*! You are the first to learn what the future really held for Cinderella.

After the ball, the prince scoured the kingdom for the mystery girl who could indeed wear the glass slipper. He felt his future depended upon it. His search became so costly that the

Exchequer of the kingdom warned him that time was running out. Cinderella was the last maiden to try the slipper and it was a perfect fit. There was a sudden swirl of silver stars and there in front of Cinderella stood her fairy godmother with a twinkle in her eye and a wand in her hand. In an instant, Cinderella was clothed in a gorgeous dress of cornflower blue silk decorated with pearls. On her feet she wore tiny white boots with blue tassels.

Immediately Cinderella recognized the creative talents of her fairy godmother. She could design dresses equal to any House of Chanel or Vera Wang creation. The shoes created would fit any size foot in the most exquisite styles, colors and design. Cinderella realized this was the opportunity that she had been yearning for: a career in business and founder of a famous House of Design. The brand "Cindy's Slippers" was her passport to fame and success. The business expanded so rapidly Cinderella and her partner, Fairy Godmother, needed substantial fortune to continue their entrepreneurial endeavor. Cinderella offered the prince a fifty percent partnership in her company.

The prince did not react like a jilted suitor. He saw the opportunity that Cinderella could bring to him, to herself, her family and her country. He became so indispensible to her that they grew her business into a conglomerate that incorporated all kingdoms in Fairyland. The exports brought untold wealth to the Prince's kingdom. Cinderella, always forgiving, seated her family members on her Board of Directors.

She realized the prince loved her for who she really was, not just her business acumen, so they were married at a wedding of the century. She was wed in one of her Vera Wang quality wedding creations and of course, glass slippers. The prince and his princess rode through the streets in a glittering golden coach shaped like a pumpkin, pulled by six white horses.

As in fairy tales of fantasy, they all lived happily ever after.

THE END

The Good Humor Man

The market crash of 1929 brought about desperate times for millions of Americans. In the previous century the Gold Rush to California had brought hope and prosperity to many. In 1930 California once again became an economic savior.

Many migrated westward in the 1930's because of the Dust Bowl, a severe dust storm in Oklahoma, Kansas, Nebraska and Eastern Colorado. Its migrating victims were called "Oakies."

During the Depression, families from my local area in Illinois went to California seeking economic success.

My information is from hearsay, eavesdropping as a girl listening to small town gossip in the 1930's. I witnessed days of dank, dusty clouds covering our skies and sun in dark shade during recess at school.

I remember when Mr. Hawkins, who went to L.A. and became a Good Humor Man, returned to visit Ridge Farm driving a fancy car. As a young girl I was impressed because the seat of the car turned to easily get out. I heard that he let it be known if anyone could make their way to California he would have a job for them. Many years later I heard that annual Ridge Farm reunions were held in California.

Here is my version of one family's flight. I tell their story in the style of the nursery rhyme, "Little Boy Blue."

Little Boy Blue

(Retold from an 18th century English nursery rhyme)

Little Boy Blue come blow your horn.

The sheep are in the meadow, the cows are in the corn.

Where is the little boy who looks after sheep?

He's not under the haystack fast asleep.

Where's that little boy that looks after sheep?

He's now a young man a fortune he seeks,

Pedaling his cart over L.A. streets.

Today Little Boy Blue delivers his wares over many city streets,

Calling for kids to buy his treats.

They come running as if under his spell,

For its Good Humor ice cream bars he has to sell.

You know that a Good Humor Man really cares

About the kids that chase after his wares.

It's the ice cream man telling his tale of how streets of L.A. echo

his call,

About how his ice cream success satisfies all.

Little Boy Blue returned to the farm,

Hoping to win with his persuasive charm.

"Come follow me, I plan to stay.

I'm that same Little Boy Blue, blowing my horn.

Calling to you, I still say,

Leave the sheep in the meadow and the cow in the corn.

For with me you'll find fortune every day

Working the streets of dear L.A."

Bedtime

(Eleanor Farjeon)

Five minutes, five minutes more, please!

Let me stay five minutes more!

Can't I just finish the castle

I'm building here on the floor?

Can't I just finish the story

I'm reading here in my book?

Can't I just finish this bead-chain –

It almost is finished, look!

Can't I just finish this game, please?

When a game's once begun

It's a pity never to find out

Whether you've lost or won.

Can't I just stay five minutes?

Well, can't I just stay four?

Three minutes then? Two minutes?

Can't I stay one minute more?

May I Have Just One Minute More?

Did you have a favorite childhood toy? A teddy bear or blanket for comfort? My brother Stanley had an imaginary companion named "Kak." My son Bruce clutched his Steiff teddy bear to his chest for so long that all semblance of plush fur was worn away!

What meaning do these things bring us in our early life? I think they represent joy, comfort, trust and belonging. Perhaps it is our first emotional attachment. Or, these objects represent our parents' love when they are not available.

Have we outgrown this connection today? I think not. The cell phone for a large segment of the population has become the toy that connects us to reality, to others and to life itself.

Baby boomers are now retired or reaching retirement. Some of us from earlier generations are in our 90s. One day while shopping at ACE Hardware for light bulbs an older gentleman next to me questioned, "Why should I buy LED light bulbs? They will live much longer than I will!"

In the last quarter of our lives we still look for the comfort of that old blanket or toy. We no longer physically seek out the object of our childhood affection, but we look for that connection to others and to love for living. We still want the joy, comfort, trust and feeling of belonging those objects represented in our childhood.

Why do terminally ill people seek out more time? Some choose to undergo complicated medical procedures and endure great pain just for the possibility of a short time more.

Seniors may ask,

"Can I finish the chore here before me?"

Just one minute more! I know I can get it done!

"May I complete this message that I haven't had a chance to give?"

I want to tell someone "I love you."

Yes we love life, this living body and spirit that we hold so dear. There is such joy in just being you.

Just one minute more, please, to say "there is such joy in being me."

I AM – now and forever more.

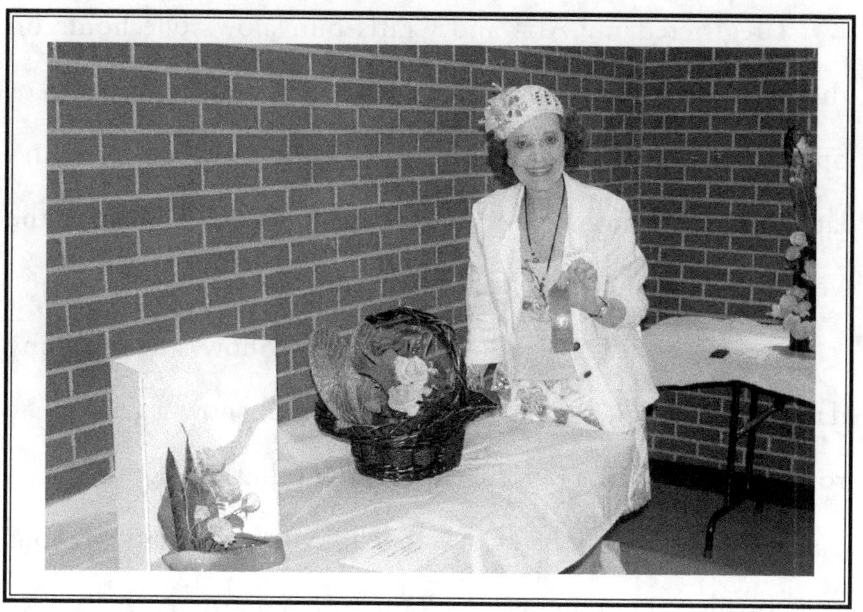

How Many Times Do I Have To Ask "What's Next?"

This journey called LIFE seems to move along as fast as a Japanese bullet train. When I become anxious about the future it stops just long enough to pick up a new answer to my question, "What's Next?"

On the road behind me 20 years of competitive ballroom dancing stretched out. Physical disabilities for the first time dictated that I stay closer to home.

I registered my Arts and Crafts bungalow style home on the National Register of Historic Places. This led to a series of open houses, historical city tours, English High Tea parties and late autumn outdoor garden fundraisers (raising funds for the Veteran's Hospital through DAR with Lynn Barnett).

By 2008 a Loveland Rose Society Show attracted my daughter's attention. She encouraged me to show a few of the roses from my heritage rose garden of 160 bushes.

Thus, another "career" developed. I won many blue ribbons and top flower arranging trophies. I served two years as Vice President and then two years as President of the Loveland Rose Society. My next goal was to become an official National Rose Society arrangement judge (yes, but I was turning 90 years old!).

I did qualify as an arrangement judge at the National Rose Show in San Diego and National Mini-Rose Show in New Jersey. By this time I was walking with a cane (as did many of my contemporaries). My daughter-in-law Debra drove me to the Rocky Mountain Regional Rose Show in Colorado Springs. Gathering together the proper paperwork, tying on a work apron, pinning on my hard earned judge's credentials, I was ready to judge my first official Regional Rose Show.

Stepping up to the table, expecting a challenge for my talents as a newly appointed judge, it did not take long to see that there were NO ENTRIES. All was not lost as Beverly Watery and Carol Macon invited us to lunch. Debra and I enjoyed an early afternoon drive back to Loveland!

Once again it was time to move on with, "What's Next?" This express train for living said, "not so fast!" You still have a deep connection with flowers. By this time I was spending the winters in Florida. I found a Japanese Ikebana Society with far stricter rules and regulations than I had encountered with the American Rose Society.

With Patricia Bonarek's encouragement I earned two levels of certification for Ikebana. Once again, my friendships were forged through our mutual love of flowers.

The next three summers (I was still travelling back and forth between Florida in the winter and Colorado in the summer) I set up all-day classes in my home. I could now share my love for and knowledge of flower arranging, incorporating American Rose Society and Ikebana design and style.

I demonstrated and lectured in the morning, we enjoyed a luncheon I hosted and in the afternoon each student created her own design from flowers she provided as I assisted and critiqued the work. My greatest satisfaction from giving these classes was that several of the participants (who themselves were ARS horticulture judges) entered their very first arrangements in an official show.

As happens to most seniors, age begins to take its toll, so much as to slow us down (by this time I was 93!). With spinal stenosis causing pain and macular degeneration causing lack of sight I asked once again, "What's Next?"

My friends, never give up. Look around, there is always a latent talent that you might have forgotten about, or your disabilities may strengthen and develop a new part of your brain. Maybe daydreaming and a "YES, I can" attitude will show you the way. At 93 I published my first book of nostalgic stories, "Grin and Giggle."

Time marches on. The bullet train keeps passing by my door, whistling, "Not yet, there is more. You still have things to do, ideas to create. Be patient. Be positive. Don't listen to your pains and disabilities." Together we can create a new horizon, a new understanding, a new beginning.

So now, at 96, I am publishing my second book dedicated

to the tenacity of seniors. The very book you are now holding in your hands. Once again I ask, "What's Next?"

To the end, I must always have the last word.

I can still look forward.

My password is HOPE.

Hope is sustaining.

It is Joy waiting.

It is Fascination.

It is Gratitude.

It is Success. Task accomplished.

It is Laughter. A smile.

It is a Surprise just around the corner.

HOPE is living with Grace and Anticipation.

What a Wonderful World!

Isn't Life GRAND!

MY GIRLS – 4 GENERATIONS

Photo Credits

Moon: <a ref="https://www.123rf.com/profile_kmiragaya">km iragaya / 123RF Stock Photo</a>

Fountain: Saadia Lababidi

Rose: Saadia Lababidi

Space: <a href="https://www.123rf.com/profile_marishaz"> marishaz / 123RF Stock Photo</a>

Doorway: Saadia Lababidi

Computer Keyboard: Saadia Lababidi

Truck: Saadia Lababidi

Donut: Saadia Lababidi

Radio Cartoon Drawing: <a href="https://www.123rf.com/profile_retroclipart"> retroclipart / 123RF Stock Photo</a>

Reading: Saadia Lababidi

Little Red Riding Hood and The Wolf: Illustration from 'Les Contes de Perrault,'Engraved by Pannemaker, published by J. Hetzel, 1862 by Gustave Dore

Gavel: <a href="https://www.123rf.com/profile_yupiramos"> yupiramos / 123RF Stock Photo</a>

Mr. Egg: <a href="https://www.123rf.com/profile_gortan123"> gortan123 / 123RF Stock Photo</a>

Tortoise and Hare: <a href="https://www.123rf.com/profile_ohyooha"> ohyooha / 123RF Stock Photo</a>

Red Roadster: <a href="https://www.123rf.com/profile_lilyoh">lilyoh / 123RF Stock Photo</a>

Bear with Hands Up: <a href="https://www.123rf.com/profile_captainvector">captainvector / 123RF Stock Photo</a>

Wolf: <a href="https://www.123rf.com/profile_cofeee">cofeee / 123RF Stock Photo</a>

House in forest: <a href="https://www.123rf.com/profile_julia700702"> Julia700702 / 123RF Stock Photo</a>

Shoe house: <a href="https://www.123rf.com/profile_aleutie">aleutie / 123RF Stock Photo</a>

All photos not specifically credited above are from the author's personal collection or from the public domain.

Ramblings and Rumblings

...and No Whining!

by Pollyann 'Pan' Castle

www.ingramcontent.com/pod-product-compliance
Lightning Source LLC
Chambersburg PA
CBHW071434100726

47908CB00004B/1153

About the Author

Pollyann Castle was born into luxury and a whirlwind of travel and activity in the Roaring 20's. The next three decades were influenced by the Great Depression, World War II and the Korean War. Her formative years were spent travelling between Ridgefarm, Illinois and Colorado.

She graduated from University of Colorado, Boulder, and University of Denver, Graduate School of Library Science; retiring after a 20 year career in education as a teacher and librarian.

Pollyann has been involved in writing and arts throughout her life. At age 10 she learned to play the cello, mail ordered from Sears and Roebuck catalog. She performed into her 80s. At 60 she began Competitive Ballroom dancing, winning national awards, recognition and trophies for over 20 years.

Pollyann organized and guided tours through Europe,

Scandinavia and the British Isles for 12 years, including extended visits to West Africa, Egypt, Turkey and the Middle East.

In Loveland, Colorado she had a heritage rose garden with 160 bushes. At 91 she qualified as American Rose Society certified Arrangement Judge for national, regional and local shows.

Her latest passion is sports (especially college basketball and football).

Her first book "Grin and Giggle" was published in 2016. Pollyann continued her creative writing, bringing to life "Mirth and Mayhem" and "Ramblings and Rumblings."

Pollyann, married twice, has 4 children, 6 grandchildren and 1 great-grandchild.

Contents

In the Beginning...

Look to the heavens on a starry night and you will see the twinkling stars and major planets blinking back at you. They want to tell you an adventurous story. Some may think it is a Tall Tale, a myth or fantasy. You can decide for yourself. Enjoy!

Commodore Cosmos, CEO of the Solar System, spent the last eon keeping an eye on and orchestrating the movements of the oldest planets in the Sun's orbit. This was tiring business, so he stopped to rest on a hidden away planet that was still to be discovered by mortals. This hidden planet, just beyond Earth and her moon, Cosmos called affectionately "Tomorrow." It represented to him the promise of hope, change, new chances and new beginnings. He had great plans for the future of planet Tomorrow.

As Commodore Cosmos stretched out and lounged, he dozed. He fell into a daydreaming state. He gazed out upon the dazzling blue planet Earth with oceans that reflected like brilliant gems. Clouds covered parts of the blue sphere and made it appear that Earth was winking at him, inviting him to take a closer look.

He asked himself, "How could I have overlooked such beauty, such color?" as the clouds formed and reformed over Earth's face.

Commodore Cosmos thought, grinning, "I do believe she is winking at me. Could she be flirting with me?" He thought for a moment that she was inviting him into her gravitational field.

Being the busy CEO of the Solar System that he was, he could not rest and linger for long. As he got up to leave and return to his duties, he spoke under his breath in a barely audible voice, "Yes, Blue Beauty, I will come to see you with gifts that will pleasure you. I may even steal a kiss or two. Unfortunately, for now I must go. Hasta La Vista, my darling."

Mars' Mayhem

One day as Earth swiveled on her axis, her blue beauty attracted Mars' attention. He began to keep an eye on her and admire her from afar. He happened to see what appeared to be Earth winking and imagined it might be intended for him.

Mars was mesmerized by Earth's heavenly beauty and magnetic charms. He was now a very cold planet, but had at one time supported life. Earth's colorful continents and rarified atmosphere touched his heart and stirred his memory of mortals on Mars.

On impulse, wishing to reach out to this Blue Beauty, Mars took a deep, deep breath and blew as hard as he could. Because of the distance, he expected his breath to enfold her in a tropical breeze, softly carrying his message. Sadly, Mars misjudged the appropriate temperature and all mayhem broke loose.

Upon contact with Earth, Mars' icy blasts formed glaciers on Earth's north and south poles. Earth's quick response was to immediately turn away from Mars, thus spurning any ideas he might have as a suitor for her attention. Mars was truly surprised and dismayed that his gesture of friendship and appreciation backfired into such chaos. He was stunned to see the havoc and blight his icy blasts caused on Earth's surface.

Wishing to make amends with an apology, Mars called out to neighboring planet Venus, Mistress of Love and Beauty, for help. Her temperament sometimes flared into a hot house atmosphere, leaving lovers to hastily throw off their clothing in a heat of passion!

However, Venus' fickle and tempestuous behavior could be tempered into a more moderate greenhouse effect. Mars believed this greenhouse effect could be sent to heal the damage he had caused. Beautiful gardens would once again cover Earth's surface.

Venus liked this idea. Together she and Mars called upon Mercury, messenger to all gods, goddesses and mortals in the Solar System. Within the Solar System, Mercury orbited closest to the Sun. At times the Sun's flares caused Mercury to forget messages, or twist and garble their delivery. Mercury's retrograde motion could cause havoc with communication.

Unfortunately, it happened again. Mercury delivered Mars' apology which produced a "hot house" effect all over all Earth. This resulted in drought and desert-like conditions drying up water sources, causing even more mayhem.

Overcome with grief and fear of further distraction, planet Earth began to cry. Her tears filled up rivers, flooded lakes and caused storms, hurricanes and tsunamis. Earth's billowing clouds and fog began to obscure her from other planets.

Mars could not believe the chain reaction of disastrous events his good intentions had created. Distraught over his actions, the only one who could help save the Blue Planet was Commodore Cosmos. It took several days of searching, but Mars finally found Cosmos at the far end of the Solar System counseling Pluto, Head of the hidden planets. As Mars arrived, Cosmos called out to him, "What's up man? How can I help?"

Mars confessed "Oh, I am so sorry!" he shouted breathlessly. "I tried to attract Earth's attention but I misjudged my strength and now she is weeping, crying uncontrollably." With great urgency Mars continued, "You must go to her for her beauty is fading rapidly. You are CEO Cosmos, I know you can console her."

Without another word or further questioning, the one who could make the impossible possible immediately started his long journey through space, hoping to save this beautiful blue planet, Earth.

When planet Earth came to the realization that crying a

river only created more destruction, she decided to stop feeling sorry for herself. It was her duty to secure and protect the living creatures that exist on her surface and she didn't want to cause further harm.

With quick, decisive determination planet Earth thought, "Why should I stand by, crying for help? I can restore my surface with focus and purpose! I know Venus will come to help. We are the only female planets in the Solar System. Let's call on our FEMALE POWER."

Venus called on goddesses and wood nymphs. With a "can do" attitude came the famed Amazon women, warriors and gladiators led by Wonder Woman.

Working together, Earth's blue beauty was restored. Her aura was shiny and bright once again. With great joy and appreciation, Earth called for a celebration.

Carnivale Di Venezia
–Party Time

Venice was chosen as the celebration site and a masquerade jubilee was planned. The St. Mark's Square was abuzz with festivities. Blue Beauty was settled on a platform where she could orchestrate the Carnival preparations. All day gods, goddesses and mortals gathered in numbers equal to a Super Bowl size arena set up for Olympic sized parades, races and marathons to honor the women who had come together to heal her.

As dusk fell across the city, lights began to twinkle, tables were set, waiters passed out appetizers and tasty tidbits. Wine and drinks flowed freely. At the end of the main San Marcos Square, the head table was surrounded by lounge chairs and couches as soft as clouds. In the center reigned planet Earth. Trumpets sounded the fanfare, "Let the Party Begin." Earth took her place as reigning Queen of her realm.

Gods, goddesses, mortals and rulers quickly gathered, many in masquerades, so few were recognized. A few uninvited guests crashed the party. Among these were Master Mars who slipped in, bringing along shy planet Pluto.

Earth sat surveying the festivities. This stunning beauty was dressed in sky blue silk chiffon. Draped across her shoulders was a shawl of gossamer white tulle as soft as a cloud. Her jet black hair was dressed with diamonds that reflected brilliance into the night's darkness, almost like beacons. Unfurled behind her was a banner that read, "There is Power in Success."

With great joy in her heart, Earth sat with her arms resting casually over the back of her chair. They were open in an inviting manner, yet signaled her strength, confidence, purpose and resolve. Her motto was "Gain loyalty through truth and trust." With rockets flaring above her, she signaled for the orchestra to begin.

The party was in full swing. Groups of masked and costumed revelers milled around talking. Others enjoyed the scrumptious banquet overflowing with bountiful dishes at beautifully decorated tables. Still others moved to the beat of the band on the dance floor.

Commodore Cosmos entered and was surprised by all the festive commotion. He had expected that Blue Beauty was still struggling with drought and blight. He had come to find a way to help her, yet here she was celebrating her healing, strength and success. This endeared him to her even more.

He decided to quietly sit at an empty banquet table and enjoy a few private moments incognito to admire her beauty. The hustling, bustling crowd did not even notice his arrival. He was dapperly dressed in goggles and early aviator attire, so he easily blended in.

As he caught sight of the Blue Beauty, his heart seemed to skip a beat. His breath came in quick succession. He had admired planet Earth from afar, but he was not expecting such beauty, mystery, unspoken power and presence to have such a visceral effect. He was utterly speechless for the first time in his life. He continued to sit as if in a trance.

Mars happened to look over and recognize Commodore Cosmos sitting alone. He wondered why the CEO of the Solar System, personage of great notoriety, was alone and unannounced at such an important occasion. Forgetting that he himself was crashing this festive scene, Mars, with Pluto closely following, boisterously approached Commodore Cosmos, blowing his cover.

The resulting commotion caught the attention of those

nearby and whispers began circulating the news which soon reached Earth. She was outraged that there were intruders at her celebration and went to confront them.

Commodore Cosmos and Mars realized at the same moment that they were both vying for planet Earth's attention. Mars had gone to find Cosmos and ask for help, but Cosmos hadn't realized all the chaos was caused because Mars had his romantic sights set on Earth. Cosmos was determined not to be outdone. Commodore Cosmos wanted to smooth over Earth's upset as quickly as possible, so he suavely asked her for a dance.

As the orchestra struck up "Some Enchanted Evening" from the musical South Pacific, Earth very reluctantly accepted Cosmos' invitation, if only to have the opportunity to admonish the party crasher more personally and privately. As the lyrics "Some enchanted evening, you may see a stranger, across a crowded room, and somehow you know, you know even then, that somehow you'll see her again and again…" played, Commodore Cosmos ushered the Blue Beauty onto the dance floor.

Mars was disappointed, but quickly recognized that there was no way he could compete with debonair Commodore Cosmos for Earth's attention, particularly in light of the chaos he had already caused her. To avoid further admonishment, he retreated to enjoy the pleasures of the party with Pluto in tow.

Earth's anger subsided much more quickly than she expected as Commodore Cosmos expertly twirled her around the dance floor with charm and grace. Soon she could hardly even remember why she had been so upset.

A Dance To Romance

The orchestra played on. Dancers stepped to the rhythm of the beat. People began noticing the sparks between Commodore Cosmos and planet Earth. Soon crowds gathered to watch the blossoming passion expressed in the dance.

As they danced, the steps, movement and rhythms reminded Cosmos that as a youth he had been a ballroom dance champion. It was not difficult for him to adjust his dance posture for the Argentine Tango. Emotions he had not recognized before began to stir in him. As he held Blue Beauty's body in the tight upper body twist, it was as if he could feel her heart beat to a rhythm of romance. He could feel her body respond, so soft and supple, that even a suggestion of movement led her in a rhythmic response to his motion.

"Your sensuous perfume envelopes me. Your magnetic attraction invites me to hold you in an endearing embrace. Your kisses have suggestions of ocean waves lapping at the shore, responding to my lips as if caressing mine. Oh, Misty Blue Beauty, you can make my every dream come true. Can you see? I adore you!" Cosmos confessed.

"Oh my darling," he continued, "I fell in love with you at first sight. I was lounging on planet Tomorrow when your heavenly blue light caught my attention. It was then that I vowed to come to you." Squeezing her hand, he smiled widely, questioning her, "Truly, were you not flirting with me? I was sure you were winking at me!"

Cosmos' sudden confession surprised both of them. It drew her response as soft repressed pleasure. A frivolous sense of abandon came over her like an impatient hurricane, wanting its way, taking control of her with passionate desires. Here was Cosmos, sweet as candy, approaching her, planet Earth, as soft as the finest breeze of summer, suggesting the promise of more embraces to come.

Cosmos could move her body across the dance floor as unexpectedly as a sudden summer thunderstorm, swirling, twirling, turning, circling, until she was as giddy as a school girl.

"Oh my sweet, will you dance with me for eternity? Our auras, our futures rely on this moment telling us we are meant for each other. Over decades of time, these beautiful things will always remind me of you. These things will bring you to me. I do declare to you, I will always be true." Cosmos pledged.

Cosmos' words touched Earth deeply for loyalty was what mattered to her above all. With this she brushed her lips across his cheek, giving his hand a little squeeze.

As the evening grew late, time slipped by into early morning, heralding the beginning of a New Dawn. Having danced the whole night through, still holding hands, the two fell together in exhausted exhilaration onto a cushy couch. It felt like they were sitting on a cloud. It had to be dancer's exhaustion that consumed them, for they had maneuvered from whirling, circling pivots to seductive hip gyrations that Latin rhythms demanded.

Sitting closely together on the couch Earth realized something was different. She asked herself, "What is this feeling? Is it a dream? Perhaps it was just the rhythm of the dance!"

"Is it just the magic of this night?" Earth asked Cosmos. "My world is continuing to spin, day is night and night becomes day. Can we meet again? Perhaps in a fortnight so we have time to process our passion?"

Hesitating for a moment Cosmos replied, "Why yes, my

Misty Blue." He was secretly very pleased she had asked. He continued, "How about meeting in Las Vegas, a city where chance makes the impossible possible? There chance and change promise new beginnings."

"Would you like a brunch on the veranda of the Bellagio Hotel where the geyser water fountains splash, spelling energy and possibilities?" Earth asked.

"We can meet there with fresh hopes and perspective," opined Cosmos. He had chosen Las Vegas as the perfect place to impress Misty Blue, for there the improbable may turn the impossible into all possibilities.

She was pleased that Cosmos accepted her proposal and understood her request for time to reflect. "OK. Let's make it a morning brunch at the Bellagio's private pavilion, an indoor-outdoor veranda where sunbeams dance and rolling breezes softly play about," agreed Earth.

Cosmos felt such relief there would be a second meeting. He would see her again and have the opportunity to ask the unspoken question he was already formulating in his mind. It was now time to go. Silence engulfed the ballroom. The band members were packing up to leave, revelers were drifting away into the darkness. Cosmos picked up Misty Blue's shawl of gossamer tulle and wrapped it around her shoulders with an irresistible caress of the long black curls cascading across her breast. Arm in arm they headed toward the Grand Canal's promenade.

Due to the early hour, they mutually decided that Cosmos would escort Misty Blue to her hotel overlooking the Grand Canal. She suggested a shortcut over the "Bridge of Sighs." The bridge historically represented the sighs of condemned criminals, but tonight it reflected the sighs of two lovers.

As they strolled along the Grand Canal's promenade, they came upon a little church where Vivaldi's violins were displayed.

"Let's go in," Cosmos suggested. Passing a display of many compositions, they quickly slid into the nearest pew. Misty Blue sat quietly beside Cosmos, each deep in contemplative thought.

Softly Cosmos started to speak, more like a whisper than spoken words, "To the maker of all creation, keeper of energy, known and unknown, I thank you for this evening, this blessed union of hearts between me and your beloved planet Blue Earth. Bless this meeting of two souls uniting in Love and Grace. Hear my prayer of gratitude–AMEN."

Reaching for Cosmos' hand, Earth gave it a light kiss, pressing his fingers to her forehead. She looked deeply, searchingly into his eyes with appreciation and for the first time, revealing her trust in him. Quietly the couple left the church, walking silently toward her hotel.

Time was moving much too fast for Cosmos and Blue Beauty. Tomorrow was just over the horizon and with the sunrise it would be today, where each had duties to perform, decisions to make, questions to ask and answers to give. The couple lingered, not wanting to say "good bye," for their kisses had become deep and hungry, fraught with emotional passion and desire.

"Well, my beauty, we must say good bye, til we meet again," Cosmos murmured. A new day was dawning.

After parting, Cosmos hurried down the avenue in the early morning light. He shouted out, "Now I know how it feels to be in love!" Cosmos could not recall any emotion in his past that had ignited his senses to such heights of attraction. He realized that now all he wanted was to hold Blue Beauty in his arms again and forever. He wanted to cherish and protect her with truth, trust and loyalty, assuring that Blue Planet Earth would flourish and develop until time itself stood still. This promise sent music to his soul. It repeated and repeated, "Yes, I hear music when I'm with you."

Cosmos was so excited about his dream of a future together he gave a high jump in the air and clicking his heels, he was off to prepare for their next meeting. It was not difficult for Cosmos to process his feeling of protection for Misty Blue that glowed with warmth and beauty in all kinds of weather, across decades and over eons of time.

It may seem odd to others that Blue Beauty did not say many words, but it always had been her duty as controller and keeper of planet Earth to listen quietly and intently to the voices of all the elements that swirl and move across Earth. She had humanity to sustain, protect and multiply...this takes a listener.

As the two parted, they each carried with them the intuitive knowledge that the enormity of what they were experiencing was much greater than either of them. Cosmos was sure of his love and devotion for Earth, knowing he was destined to take care of her, protect her and comfort her in adversity.

When Misty Blue returned to her room just before the morning sunrise, she approached this unexpected tryst from a different angle; she had very different responsibilities to consider. Her responsibility was to sustain and protect the living, breathing, productive life forms on earth. This, in conjunction with Gravity. Gravity shields the five elements (space, earth, air, water, and fire) from the rigors and weightlessness of outer space.

Misty Blue sat in her boudoir lounge in deep reminiscence. She had been a mentor and guardian angel to mortal women of power and influence. Earth pondered what advice she would give herself.

Cosmos' words of discovery and endearment touched her heart deeply. To have such a worldly, powerful man profess love and attraction to her was a new experience. Yes, she did have lovers in the past, but Cosmos' words and emotions had a different urgency and vibration to them. She was so mesmerized by his emotional plea, she wished to hear more. Besides, the dancing only ignited her mounting ardent attraction as their bodies had glided about the ballroom floor.

It was complete rhapsody of emotions that they were surrendering to. "How could this happen? He is CEO of the Solar System with the power and decisiveness of a commanding Officer, a "Mr. Fixit," she mused. Cosmos, who leads with a steady hand and decisive analysis of a situation was moved by his meeting with her, planet Earth. "How could this happen?" she asked again with a smile.

Blue Beauty's question to herself was, "Would marriage affect my relationship with the mortals, elements and nature I oversee?" Finally, the excitement of the previous night clouded her senses. In her drowsy state she thought she could hear Cosmos calling to her. His words seemed to float through the open window like a caressing gentle breeze.

As if she heard his words, she responded, "Yes, I hear your heart's desire. My heart too, pulsates to the rhythm of our romance. I have been moved by our kisses, your whispers in my ears, your caresses and the longing invitation in your eyes. It speaks the pulsating rhythm of love for me," she confessed to herself as she drifted off to sleep.

Peeking in my windows,
Knocking at my door,
Your Force feels free to enter
    Yet Uninvited-
    Still Unknown-
    Unrecognized.
This masked stranger named Fascination
Keeps calling out, tapping at my senses.
Reminding, refreshing, repeating
"See me, smell me, taste me,
Hear my whispers in your ear, know my touch.

Not yet, I say, my front door is closed for sleep.
My eyelids shuttered by the darkness of slumber,
I'm unaware of New Beginnings being offered.

And again, once more there starts a rapping, a tapping
That allows a pleasurable opening of my chamber door.
It is the breeze, softly, silently pulsating.

There my body has been prepared to receive in a room of Silence.
Waiting, throbbing, quivering, yearning, calling out

Come In. Come In. Come In.

I am here, waiting, wondering,

How did you find me?

How did you know my name?

Misty Blue, Misty Blue…..You keep calling…..Misty Blue.

Yes, Yes, I feel your presence, I know your name.

You are my muse, my dearest deepest knowing.

Come to me with your boundless Joy,

Shower me wih your fruits of Youth.

You are the maker of Possibilities—opening my doors and

Pleasuring me with magic forces.

Come lie beside me.

You are my muse, you are the giver of everlasting love.

A Gamble In Las Vegas

Commodore Cosmos wasted no time getting to Las Vegas. He wanted to set the stage for the next meeting with Blue Beauty and wanted everything perfect. He kept asking himself, "What can I do that will please, surprise and entertain the tempestuous longing in Blue Beauty's heart? She must see me as trustworthy and loyal. My heart is full of everlasting love and I want her to recognize it in every detail."

Commodore Cosmos went directly to the Bellagio Hotel on the strip in Vegas. He contacted the hotel event planner because he intuitively believed that by engaging living, breathing, productive people on planet Earth, she would see his true love for her in action.

So, to work they went. The head chef was consulted to plan a brunch that introduced exotic and delicious dishes from around the globe. Florists were to decorate the room befitting a royal occasion. There would be flowering trees with twinkling lights and exotic birds nesting in the higher branches. Floating about the ceiling would be colorful balloons and kites, mimicking clouds playing in a blue sky. Sprays of orchids in all shapes and colors would lushly adorn the tables. The flowers would create an exotic, exciting perfume of anticipation - a garden kaleidoscope of changing color. A bouquet of red and white roses was to be prepared to gift Blue Beauty at the table.

Cosmos called for a small chamber orchestra to be discretely placed in a side alcove. They would play baroque music with quick tempo, sudden changes and riffling of the instruments up and down the scale to elicit stirring emotions. The chamber orchestra would softly serenade Misty Blue's entry with the song dear to the two of them, "I Could Have Danced All Night."

As a special tribute to the touching moment they had shared at the Vivaldi Church, he chose Vivaldi's "Four Seasons" to be played during the meal. Across the room, representing another musical era, he requested a jazz band to play love songs of the Big Band craze that had swept the world. Another tribute and salute to human creativity and high spirit.

Behind a stage curtain, a stone cutter from South Africa would be waiting with an exquisite engagement ring showcasing a diamond of exceeding size and beauty, a hope diamond should she say "Yes" to Cosmos' planned proposal of marriage.

The fortnight passed quickly for Cosmos with so many details to address in preparation for the agreed upon reunion with Misty Blue. At the same time, it felt like an eternity had passed since he had held Blue Beauty in his arms and twirled her around the dance floor.

Cosmos understood the enormity of the question he would ask Misty Blue and the importance of her response. Only she had it within her power to make all of his dreams come true. He reflected that his heart was pure, his intentions noble. His promises would be everlasting. He asked for the Fates of Good Fortune to shine favorably on this occasion.

The big day finally arrived. Cosmos was early to review every detail one last time. Yes, his scene was set for celebration.

Commodore Cosmos, satisfied that everything was in order, sat down at their table set exquisitely for two to wait for her arrival. He had been absent from his CEO duties for too long, so in these moments of quiet anticipation he took out his appointment calendar and became engrossed with his "To Do" list.

Misty Blue, a vision of springtime, stepped into the enchanted scene that Cosmos had orchestrated. Her dress, as white as her earthly glaciers, flared out as she walked. Kick pleats of flaming, fiery red flickered and swirled as she moved. The wide brim of her hat lifted and fluttered seductively across her eyes as she walked onto the private veranda. Her red stiletto heels tapped in anticipation.

Blue Beauty saw Cosmos in deep concentration, consumed by work. In that moment he appeared vulnerable, relaxed and at ease. This amused her and she giggled silently just as she stepped into a shaft of sunlight, giving her a glowing aura.

At that exact moment Commodore Cosmos looked up to see this vision of beauty, grace and poise, glowing in the sunlight. The sight took his breath away. He gulped for air as he rose to greet her.

Blue Beauty stepped willingly into Cosmos' open arms. Their eyes locked and lips met in a kiss as familiar and sweet as it was full of promise. As he seated her across the table from him, his thoughts dwelled on the kiss they had just shared. Encouraged, he thought it bode well for a positive response to his planned overtures.

Commodore Cosmos picked up a long stemmed red rose in full bloom. Pressing it into her hands he said with yearning in his eyes, "This my dear, represents the fire that is in my heart. It carries a kiss from my lips to yours."

She accepted the red rose, holding it to her nose so she could inhale the sweet, sensuous perfume coming from the heart of the open blossom. Looking up at Cosmos she responded, "This red rose celebrates the passion that has been ignited by our love."

Smiling, Cosmos picked up the white rose and placed it across the plate in front of her. "I give you this white rose that celebrates the virginal purity of our romance. We have experienced and shared our hearts and a trust that is overflowing with adoration and love."

They raised flutes of the finest champagne in a toast, as if to seal their unity.

Tea For Two

Cosmos and Misty Blue had been talking for hours, telling each other of their hopes, ambitions, yearnings and wishes. The chamber orchestra left and the marble floor was cleared so that ample space opened up for Cosmos' expert dance steps. To relieve the seriousness of their conversation, they felt the need to move, to dance. Signaling a lively foxtrot from the dance band, Cosmos took Misty Blue into his arms and they glided across the floor. Earth could match Cosmos' strong waltz with quick circular fleckerels, but most favored by both of them was the American Foxtrot. As a tease, the band leader switched to a Latin number where the hips rotated forward with every step change, and with the hand pressure, Cosmos could lead her circling around him where he could enjoy her flirting, teasing, "come get me" suggestions in the heat of the Latin dance.

The American Foxtrot once again brought their bodies close together so that with flexed knee pushing pressure against her thigh, tilting her pelvis forward and lifting her breast forward, he could go as fast or slow as the music suggested. When she lifted her breast to feel his body lead he could direct her motion from side to side. As their bodies swayed in rhythm, cheek to cheek with her hand in his, he could fold it into his side as in a light embrace. In this closed amorous position, he could feel her full ample breast pressing to his chest.

Playing the song, "Tea for Two" rumba style, the band leader signaled dessert was ready. The music ended, all was silent. As Cosmos softly brushed across her eager lips, he held her with his arms about her shoulders. She eagerly accepted his head and shoulders pressing closer and closer to her. Their passion was sealed—it was if they had always known each other over the eons.

Back at their table, the pastry chef was preparing a flaming Bananas Foster, every bit as hot and fiery as their passion on the dance floor. The band softly orchestrated the moment Cosmos would ask the important question that would seal their fates. The vocalist started singing a popular love song. Lingering on the dance floor, longing to feel their hearts beating as one together, they clung to each other as if to carry their devotion for each other through eternity.

Drawing away from Cosmos' embrace so as to catch her breath, Misty Blue looked into his eyes, and the emotional magnetism held her gaze until she felt as if she had plunged to the depth of his soul. Time stood still in this majestic moment. Silence engulfed the room. All stood as if hypnotized.

With uncharacteristic behavior, Misty Blue reached for the microphone that the singer held and started to softly sing a love song. When the lyrics of the verse came to "I love you," she stopped and looked again into Cosmos' gaze. She choked back an emotional gasp, leaned forward so they were face to face, and repeated softly with surprise in her voice as if this was the first time she admitted, even to herself, that she was now and forever steadfastly in love with this man. "Yes, I love you," she repeated in jubilation, reaching out her arms as if to embrace the entire solar system, "Cosmos my dearest, will you marry me? I commit my heart, my soul, my eternity to your care. I LOVE YOU." And with this unexpected confession, her knees buckled. She collapsed into Cosmos' arms crying uncontrollably and whispered, "Oh what have I done? Oh Cosmos, please forgive my forwardness." She was shaking with uncertainty.

"Oh my precious," he responded softly, wanting to reassure her. Her bold declaration and question was an unexpected surprise. Still processing the enormity of her entreaty, he continued, "I am fascinated by the power, spirit and determination that you pledged your heart, your future, your very destiny to me."

Cosmos dropped onto one knee and signaled the South African jeweler to produce the dazzling diamond ring. "No matter what the eons bring for us, I declare and promise to be always faithful, trustworthy, truthful and loyal to you and your earthly challenges. I promise you I will be true to you til the end of time. My heart is pure and my desires endless. I must confess, I love you my Misty Blue. I endow you with all of the blessings that I can give. Will you accept my gifts, my love, and my promise? Misty Blue, Ruler of Planet Earth, will you marry me? "

Tears of joy filled her eyes as she answered, "Yes, I will marry you." She continued, "Your swagger and bravado in San Marcos sent chills and thrills through my very core. I know now that you HAD me with our first dance. The electricity of my hand in yours, the vibration of the music matched the swing and sway of our bodies moving as one. The love lyrics that you sang in my ear, the touch of our cheeks caressed such desire. Yes, my darling, I am yours. I love you. I give you my heart. I will marry you!"

Cosmos tenderly slipped the shimmering diamond onto her finger, kissing her hand and then kissing her deeply on the lips.

Cosmos led his now betrothed to the open Bellagio veranda where the fountains geysered streams of water dancing, twirling and whirling into the air accompanied by the triumphant celebration of the "Hallelujah Chorus" from Handel's Messiah. Cosmos shouted to the Las Vegas strip and to the world, "She said YES!"

Cosmos had even more surprises planned. Walking arm in arm, they arrived at the street below, greeted by an atmosphere of mirth and expectant jubilation. Cosmos had arranged for a repeat of the Pasadena Rose Parade. The theme for the parade and interpreted by each float was, "She said YES!"

Cosmos escorted Misty Blue to the lead car where the parade Grand Marshal waited to officially begin the parade. Once again Cosmos turned to Misty Blue on one knee, took her hand and asked in proper fashion, "My dearest, my love, will you marry me?"

"Yes, yes, yes!" she replied. Over the loudspeaker the parade Grand Marshal announced, "She said YES! Let the celebration begin!" The crowd broke out in a joyous cheer. Airplanes flew overhead with banners furling behind them carrying the message, "She said YES!"

As Time Goes By

Cosmos and Misty Blue settled into married life and time passed quickly for the newlyweds. Misty Blue lay in Cosmos' arms at night and he gazed at his sleeping beauty, her head resting on his shoulder. Cosmos thought to himself, "How could I have been so lucky? She said 'yes' forever and ever." His thoughts wandered to his dream to awaken the planet Tomorrow, a dream he now shared with his wife, a dream they could fulfill together. Cosmos lovingly patted Misty Blue's growing belly as he drifted off to sleep. His last thought as he joined her in slumber was, "You will soon be 'Mother Earth' my dear one. Yes, there is hope for Tomorrow."

Cosmos, caught up in his duties as CEO of the Solar System, was required to travel for extended periods of time. He was ever true to his beloved Misty Blue and they exchanged letters whenever he was away.

My Baby Blue,

"When I hear that serenade in blue, I'm somewhere in another world alone with you. Sharing all the joys we used to know, may moons ago."

To you I will always be true. I am far away in space, but before my eyes I see your fascinating face. You are my greatest prize.

Your ever loving husband,
Cosmos

Dearest Cosmos,

I miss the comfort of your arms around me. Climate change, waters rising over shores, our beloved Venice sinking into the sea are all daily concerns. My surface is ever changing but my mortals seem capable of overcoming any adversity.

Your last visit was much too short. Our son Kallitt and I miss you constantly. Come home soon. I'll be waiting with open arms and open heart.

Your loving wife,
Mother Earth

My dearest Mother Earth,

You will always be Misty Blue to me.

At times the space that separates us is almost too much to bear. It has been too long since we were last together. My work here, jumping from planet to planet putting out fires, leaves me empty — body, mind and soul. I need you next to me. You comfort and renew me. Your beauty brightens my day. Come my dear, in our sweet dreams let's reunite and rekindle our romance.

Kiss my tired eyes, run your fingers through my hair, smoothing it back so you can whisper in my ear. As your breath sweeps a soft awakening breeze across my body, your caress and your hands sliding over me send bolts of lightening to my very core. Oh my precious wife I can hardly wait to share your fiery hot passion once again. I promise I will be home again soon.

Yours forever,

Cosmos

Will Dreams Come True?

Kallitt, son of Commodore Cosmos and Mother Earth, worked long hours helping mortals solve all kinds of problems and dilemmas. He was gaining a reputation as a well respected and sought after counselor. The long hours and weight of all the problems he helped solve left him feeling exhausted. He attempted to relieve the constant tiredness with frequent, short vacations. However, the party, party, party lifestyle of the singles he knew who had the time and resources to accompany him left him feeling even more tired and empty. It also accentuated the nagging feeling of loneliness that afflicted him. Although he had many friends and acquaintances, ultimately, he was alone.

Kallitt's mother, Planet Earth, had always been his advisor and mentor. With this current matter he decided he would approach his father Cosmos, CEO of the Solar System. He wanted to see if Cosmos had some manly insight and might approve of some extended time off.

Kallitt approached his father and explained his concerns. Commodore Cosmos responded to Kallitt, "Yes, my son, you do work hard, and it is appreciated. However, you party hard, too. I know the private clubs you frequent, and the celebrities you hang out with on Earth." Kallitt had never heard his father speak so sternly to him before.

Then with Cosmos' voice rising, "You spend way too much time with Bacchus, Ruler of Wine and Drink. Your Mother and I have great expectations and dreams for you, my son."

Kallitt tried to explain to his father how empty these things made him feel. Cosmos continued, "Putting all of this aside, I do agree that you need a break, perhaps with new vistas and a chance to meet someone to help you take your mind off your work and your loneliness. Your Mother and I have a very dear friend, Pannay, the Ruler of Color and Rainbows. She is a fiery redhead who is sophisticated, yet fun loving and playful. Wherever she goes, sweet perfume precedes her arrival. She is responsible for the colors and perfumes in all of nature."

Kallitt's spirits immediately brightened. He was ready for any adventure that would please his father.

Unbeknownst to Kallitt, Cosmos had been grooming his son to inherit and rule a special planet (yet unknown to mortals) in the solar system. First Cosmos wanted Kallitt to prove his worthiness, loyalty and character. Kallitt had a growing reputation as a counselor, but other aspects of his character still concerned Cosmos. Cosmos had consulted with planet Saturn, Ruler of Discipline. Together they had formulated a plan to test Kallitt. It was now time to put their plan into action. Introducing Kallitt to Pannay would provide the perfect opportunity to test Kallitt's resolve and character.

Commodore Cosmos spoke with persuasion, "Pannay is just the companion you are looking for. She lives in a little house on a hillside where sensuous, fun loving, joyous creatures abound. These are created in the mind and brought into being by the element Fire."

"I have one further request, Kallitt," cautioned Cosmos. "She deserves the finest companion in this playground of whimsical amusement. You must promise not to break her heart."

"How will I find her? Will I recognize her?" quizzed Kallitt.

"You may not know that she is your intended companion," replied Cosmos.

"I do not understand," Kallitt frowned. "I don't have patience for playing games. My days are filled with counseling and fixing mortal lives."

"Alright, here is a magic compass shaped with an outline of lips. When the compass finds this image on her body she will open her eyes, recognizing your charm, talents and purity of purpose."

With a pat on Kallitt's back, Cosmos admonished, "Take it slow, my good man, breath deeply so you can find and enjoy the regeneration that you and Pannay will share. Now, be on your way toward the East where a Second Sunrise is waiting for you to discover a New Beginning."

Kallitt travelled for days, searching mountain valleys and rolling hillsides. Finally one day, quite unexpectedly, he saw far in the distance a little thatch roofed bungalow covered with climbing red roses. With a light tap, he knocked on the door, but there was no answer. He ever so gently pushed the door open and in a soft whisper called out, "Pannay? Pannay?"

There was still no answer. With another step or two he could see around the room. There, tucked away in a far corner, was a woman who fit Cosmos' description of Pannay. She was fully stretched out on a sofa bed with long red tresses cascading across the pillow. She was sound asleep.

Elated that he had finally found her, Kallitt kissed Pannay's forehead. He blew softly into her ear, and tapped her heart-trust three times, trying to wake her up, but nothing worked.

From his pocket, Kallitt took out the magical compass that points to the true compassion of the heart. He blew three times into the engraved shape of a kiss emblazoned on the compass. The compass flew directly to Pannay's heart. On her breast was an exact match of the image on the compass. Kallitt pressed the compass to her breast and Pannay slowly opened her eyes. She knew it would be her destiny to play in the garden of relaxed magic. She gathered around her nude body the garments that she would need in her new state of awareness. It was magical that she could once again titillate, entertain and frolic in a playground known only to herself and her new companion.

Kallitt and Pannay entered the magical playground called Imagination together. Kallitt found Pannay to be everything his father Cosmos had promised and more. Her fiery nature provided inspiration, excitement and spontaneity.

Time passed. Here, in this midsummer's night drama, secrets were softly whispered to each other, creating magical dances. Kallitt and Pannay sat side by side, sharing mythical sensuous beginnings to their own story, dreaming of creating their own Shangri-La.

In the early mist of a new morning's dawn, just before sunrise, a buzzing swarm of mosquitoes preceded Commodore Cosmos, announcing his arrival. His very presence suggested to the two that he had a serious message. It was a proclamation, a warning of sorts.

Cosmos picked up the right hand of each of them, clasping them in his, and looked Kallitt in his eyes. He gave them his warning. "You two may have created a Royal Playground of unbridled laughter, giggles and exalted happiness, but without commitment there is no future. Hope must be genuine and trust must be secure."

Cosmos had been watching these two very closely for he saw a great future for them. "Should your enthusiasm and passions overflow into human physical passion and lust, then this spell will be broken. The shared devotion that you now hold for each other will vanish, blown away by the North Wind, never to be found again. Your Playground will then be known as the land of broken promises. If trust and expectations are compromised, hearts are broken. Chilling winds of change will blow across the human spirit. Lives will alter. Hope will be crushed."

Kallitt and Pannay were stunned, not realizing themselves that they were at the brink of falling in love. It was a moment of truth. Would they now heed the warning?

Cosmos awaited their choice. "Promises are to be kept. Hold a promise close to your heart. Keep it safe."

Kallitt and Pannay looked at each other in dismay and disbelief, both realizing that they had work to do. Kallitt needed to get back to his counseling duties and spring was advancing rapidly, requiring Pannay's magic touch. They decided it was time to part. "Oh Kallitt," Pannay suggested, "Let's celebrate the time we had together with a poem I dedicated to us."

I Want—I WANT

I want a golden cage, so fine,
Larger than a king size bed.
It's really for a friend of mine
Cause this is where I want him led.

> *Male peacock tails adorn the top,*
> *And each feather's eye will flicker and wink*
> *Until the late night breezes slowly stop,*
> *Allowing him to sleep after one last blink.*

Downey ostrich plumes make-up his bed

Keeping him from morning's dew,

Tickling his face he turns his head

To ask me "Can this all be true?"

> *Yes, my darling, you ARE my pet.*
>
> *But to keep you happy, I'll use my wiles,*
>
> *(Please now, dear SHH! Not one regret.)*
>
> *Would chocolate bon-bons keep your smiles?*

Think perfume and powder, sherry and lace.

Could this or more please your taste??

So that one fine day, you would sing a tune

Declaring to me "Oh No, 'tis not a waste,

AND much more FUN than some other place."

Kallitt, although surprised, felt a sense of relief. The time they had spent together was heartfelt and wonderful, but he certainly did not wish to commit to any bond, promise or vow just now. It was time to go.

Pannay stood in her cottage doorway, yearning for a last goodbye, one last kiss. As she reluctantly headed back into the cottage, she saw that Kallitt had forgotten the lip-shaped compass that had awakened her. Pannay ran back out hoping to catch Kallitt and cried out, "You forgot your compass." In that moment, as she reflected on the time they had shared together, Pannay realized that she had fallen in love with Kallitt.

Weathering the Storm

Kallitt hurried away, suddenly anxious to get back to his duties. After several days of travel he found himself to be absently wandering about without purpose, deep in thought.

After hours of aimless wandering Kallitt sat down to rest under a spreading chestnut tree. He wanted to sort out his tumultuous thoughts and feelings. He had expected to leave Pannay without looking back.

Suddenly, he heard girlish laughter, splashing water and screams of delight. Then he recognized a male voice. It was Pan, a companion of the nymphs and sprites. Pan saw Kallitt and brought his party over to where Kallitt was resting. "Come on over. A good swim will pack up all of your troubles!" declared Pan as he impishly pushed Kallitt toward the lake.

Bare breasted water nymphs and sprites were climbing a cliff and sliding down a waterfall. Wood nymphs, running in and out among the trees at the edge of the lake, played hide and seek.

In the meantime, Pannay was having trouble getting motivated to spread the joy of Spring. "Oh Kallitt," Pannay lamented. "You left thinking we were through. It was just a dalliance for you. After you were gone I was shocked and surprised to find that I miss you. You are in my daydreams and in my dreams at night. Your smile, your touch, your caresses and kisses linger in my heart and mind. My dearest Kallitt, I fell in love with you."

Pannay decided she needed to get Kallitt off her mind and the best way to accomplish that would be to get busy. Instead of sulking and feeling sorry for herself, she was determined to get the colors and scents of Spring spread across the land.

Pannay set to work, brightening the world with her rainbow

colors. She travelled hither and yon. Suddenly, she heard melodious laughter and peeked through the bushes to see water nymphs and sprites frolicking about. Pan was seated at the edge of a lake and another figure sat next to him in the shadow of a tree. Could it really be Kallitt? Pannay's heart fluttered, skipped a beat and then felt like it had shattered into a million pieces. It definitely was Kallitt.

In total shock, Pannay slipped away. She was overwhelmed with whirling emotions. She felt FURIOUS, broken hearted and betrayed. Pannay retreated to her cottage and locked the door tightly. Throwing herself upon her bed, she fell into a trance-like slumber.

Meanwhile, Kallitt could not get thoughts of Pannay and their time together out of his mind. Not even the bare breasted nymphs had distracted him for more than a cursory glimpse.

He decided he needed to pull himself together. Focusing on work once again would help him forget Pannay and put things in perspective. Kallitt began dealing with the huge backlog of problems that had piled up in his absence.

Returning to work didn't have the effect Kallitt had expected. Instead of taking his mind off Pannay, he became more and more despondent with each passing day. Finally, he decided the only thing that would make him feel better was to go see Pannay. Was her time with him just a passing dalliance as her poem had suggested? Did she miss him at all? Did she miss him as much as he missed her? Was she ready or willing to make a commitment if he was? He felt only going to see her and talking to her would provide insight and answers to all the questions swirling in his head.

Once again, Kallitt took time off from work. He set off in search of Pannay. This time he knew his way–he just had to follow his heart.

When Kallitt arrived at Pannay's cottage it was overgrown with wilting, withering weeds. He knocked on the door and there was no answer. He called out, but there was no response. He tried to open the door, but it was tightly locked. Could she have left and gone somewhere, or was she inside? Why was everything in such disarray?

Becoming increasingly alarmed and distressed, he sat down on the little porch to collect himself. He decided to try to find another way to get in. He began to check the windows and found a window just slightly open. He was able to open it far enough to squeeze through.

As Kallitt's eyes adjusted to the darkness inside the cottage, memories of the time he had spent here with Pannay flooded him. His heart quickened when he saw her sleeping, her fiery red hair splayed across the bed. Quickly scanning the room, his eyes settled on the compass lying on her bedside table.

He had used the compass once to wake her up. Would it work again? He blew into the magical compass three times and then placed it on her breast. Pannay's eyes fluttered open. She reached out, pulling Kallitt into a passionate embrace. Their lips met in a kiss of promise and hope for new beginnings. Looking deep into Pannay's eyes, Kallitt declared his eternal love and commitment to her.

Commodore Cosmos was elated with the turn of events. He jubilantly shared the news with Mother Earth. They both had great expectations for Kallitt and Pannay.

The betrothal was announced throughout the solar system. The wedding would be held in Westminster Abbey on New Year's Day. The news was met with a spirit of joyous expectation. All over planet Earth, celebrations spontaneously broke out encircling the globe. From outer space planet Earth seemed to be aglow. Preparations began and teams worked fervently for months in preparation for the BIG DAY.

Hope Springs Eternal

What a day of celebration it had been! Kallitt and Pannay's wedding ceremony had been beautifully touching, brimming with emotion. They had greeted hundreds of well wishers in the receiving line. The banquet, catered by the most famous chefs, had been exquisite. The day had been flawless; the music and dancing, toasts of the finest champagne raised in congratulation, a dessert buffet to marvel the eye and palette and an enormous wedding cake as a grand finale.

Symbolic gifts from the elements added a special touch to the day. Intricate ice sculptures decorated the banquet tables, representing the gift of Water. Colorful hot air balloons filled the sky, providing a dramatic backdrop representing the gift of Air. Pannay wore a brilliant tiara of fine jewels representing the gift of Earth. After dusk, a dazzling pyrotechnic display represented the gift of Fire.

After the festivities had drawn to a close, Kallitt, Pannay, Mother Earth and Father Cosmos rode through the streets in a horse drawn carriage to the family estate. They quickly settled in the familiar and comfortable library. The men shed their formal ties and jackets while the ladies kicked off their heels and released their formal coiffures into cascades of relaxed curls and waves.

Cosmos, always a lover of music, selected a Braham's symphony on the sound system. Mother Earth lit the many candles about the room until a soft glow flickered and danced around the little family. Kallitt set logs ablaze in the large stone fireplace, while Pannay poured flutes of champagne.

Cosmos, standing before the glowing embers of the fire, lifted his glass, tipping it in salute to the newlywed couple. Addressing them he said, "My dearest children, Mother Earth and I carry the deepest heartfelt love for both of you that any parent can hold. We have worked all of our lives for this moment so we could give you a home for eternity." He finished with a choked voice, "You know this."

Cosmos was overcome with emotion, as the weeks and years away from his beloved wife and the sacrifices they had both endured suddenly weighed heavy. Brushing a tear from his eye he continued, "Saturn and all the planets of the Solar System have been waiting for this day as well. My dearest children, we all bestow upon the two of you a new home for you to settle, perpetuate and propagate with all the wonders and benefits of Planet Earth. We give you planet Tomorrow."

"Yes, my darlings," continued Mother Earth. "You will take with you the magical magnetic life giving elements that support and assure life as mortals know it." Tears welled up in her eyes as she went to Cosmos, wanting to feel his warm embrace reassure her.

Pannay understood the enormity of this gift, for her rainbow of renewal and good fortune could not serve or survive without Earth's elements. Pannay rose from the couch and hurried over to Cosmos and Mother Earth, kissing each one on the cheek. She held her glass high in a gesture of acceptance, "Our hearts are overflowing."

Slipping his arm around Pannay's waist, Kallitt raised his glass, "A toast to you, Mother and Father, for this day has been your dream since you, Father Cosmos, first set sight on Mother, planet Earth, from planet Tomorrow. I understand the sacrifices you have both endured in order to give us this gift." Kallitt saluted again in a special tribute to his Mother, "With our greatest gratitude and appreciation we accept and take with us to our new home, planet Tomorrow, the five elements that will ensure a second home for Earth's mortals and all living creatures. Tomorrow promises New Beginnings. It is the place where hope springs eternal for on Tomorrow the future is NOW."

The four of them raised their glasses together to toast the new beginning.

THE END

Photo Credits

Space with bright star: <ahref="https://www.123rf.com/profile_marishaz">marishaz / 123RF Stock Photo</a>

Bellagio and fountains: <ahref="https://www.123rf.com/profile_yooranpark">yooranpark / 123RF Stock Photo</a>

Inside Bellagio: <ahref="https://www.123rf.com/profile_kobby_dagan">kobby_dagan / 123RF Stock Photo</a>

Fireworks: <ahref="https://www.123rf.com/profile_neilld">neilld / 123RF Stock Photo</a>

Westminster Abbey: <ahref="https://www.123rf.com/profile_coward_lion">coward_ion / 123RF Stock Photo</a>

Horse drawn carriage: <ahref=https://www.123rf.com/profile_Baloncici >Baloncici / 123RF Stock Photo</a>

All photos not specifically credited above are from the author's personal collection or from the public domain.

My heartfelt appreciation goes to the hard working team that brought this book from ideas in my head to the printed page you now hold in your hands.

L to R:

Debra Schneider, Editor

Nancy Schewe, Scribe

Pollyann Baird, Author

Lynn Kitchen, Publisher